The Last Day of Ramadan

A Novel by
Gandharva raja

Gandharva raja,
with Amanita Books
Columbia, Maryland

Copyright 2019 by Dr. Tapendu K. Basu

All rights reserved. No part of this book may be reproduced or transmitted in any form or by any means without written permission of the author.

This is a work of fiction. Any resemblance to any particular person or place is strictly coincidental.

Published by Gandharva raja through Amanita Books, an imprint of Summit Crossroads Press, sumcross@aol.com.

Website: Gandharvaraja.com

ISBN: 978-0-9991565-3-7

Library of Congress Control Number:2019905842

Cover Design: SelfPubBookCovers.com/Dmick27
Interior design by Eileen McIntire

Books by Gandharva raja

Hoofbeats: Song of You, A Poetic History of the United States
Epic Mahabharata: A Twenty-first Century Retelling
August 29: How Kabir H. Jain Became a Deity
Nisha Trilogy
The Last Day of Ramadan
I, Kanishka: The Author and the Emperor

Dedication

To my family, my father, and my mother for their love;

To men and women of courage who fight for individual and collective liberty;

To politicians who strive to achieve equal opportunity for all;

To journalists who die to preserve our right to freedom of expression;

To nine-year-old Thita,

who on our revisit of Yangon four days after our first landing

in Myanmar in 2005 came running to say, "I remember you.

You bought cards from me for two thousand Kiat. Here is a free gift for you."

I accepted Thita's gift of a picture postcard with a bow.

As my daughter and I crossed the street in front of Shule Paya,

I felt Buddha loved me.

Acknowledgments

The concept prevails in poetry that nothing is truly original—that each new verse is derived from a previously developed theme by the progenitor poet. Each book is another page in the epistemic evolution of man's search for truth, and through it, peace.

Wisdom takes its cue as much from the modern scientist as from the ancient texts. *The Vedas* (Patrick Olivelle, *Upanishads*, Oxford University Press: 1996), the *Old Testament* and *New Testament* (New Living Translation, *Holy Bible*, Tyndale House Publishers, Illinois: 1997), and the *Koran* (N. J. Dawood, *The Koran*, with A Parallel Arabic Text, Penguin Books, London: 1995) are prominent among the seminal texts of religious philosophy. Philosophy and metaphysics evolved with the "the axial people" of ancient Greece, Mesopotamia, Palestine, China, and India (Karen Armstrong, T*he Great Transformation: The Beginning of Our Religious Traditions*, Alfred A. Knopf, New York: 2006). Karen Armstrong's introspective commentary on the evolution of Judaism and the "Jesus Movement" (Karen Armstrong, *The Bible,* Atlantic Monthly Press, New York: 2007) provides thoughtful reading. Donald W. Mitchell introduces the Buddhist experience with the authority of a three-decade truth seeker and a professor (Donald W. Mitchell, *Buddhism: Introducing the Buddhist Experience*, 2nd. ed., Oxford University

Press, New York: 2008).

Armstrong's "immaculately researched new biography of Muhammad" truly has a "genuine relevance to the global crises we face today" (Karen Armstrong, *Muhammad,* HarperCollins Publishers, New York: 2006). Religion is the river that flows through a society and nourishes it. A river will gather silt. Bert Ehrman examines possible apocryphal inclusions in the New Testament (Bert Ehrman, *Misquoting Jesus*, HarperCollins Publishers, New York: 2005).

I owe a great deal to Professor Emeritus Donald Gibson, Department of English, Rutgers University, and Elmira Wilkey of Bishop McNamara High School, Bourbonnais, Illinois, for their editorial advice and persevering encouragement.

Freethinkers have remodeled staid edifices, nowhere more so in modern times than the Enlightenment in Europe (Norman Hampson, *The Enlightenment,* Penguin Books: Middlesex, England: 1986). The rest of the world must rethink old beliefs. Freethinkers are not iconoclasts; they repair and reface the icons.

The author acknowledges all who place humanity above parochial and patriotic interests. There is no peace without justice and no justice without truth.

Preface

The world remains in turmoil. A ferocious tug-of-war is being waged across a philosophical divide. Our life, liberty, and the pursuit of happiness are at stake. Who is the next deity that will bring peace and harmony to this enraged world? Who will douse the flames of religious extremism and rising intolerance—the world over and in the United States?

We worship God restricted by the bungee cord of organized religion. Religion is the safe ticket to our reserved orchestra seats in heaven, to a higher station at rebirth or our private harem in paradise stocked with ten virgins. As I write this book, I ask what religion means and what it should mean—to the individual and to humankind. Organized religion can do us much good and much harm. Consider the crusade and the jihad. Organized religion is divisive for reasons that benefit a few—the media-savvy clergy, politicians who nibble on our inborn insecurity, and warlords who wolf down our fears.

I want to know what soul is. Does soul exist? Is soul the God particle that lives in every living being? Who will fight for our soul, our life, our liberty, and our pursuit of happiness? All fights are of the spirit—the body merely the spirit's shield. Can Jain, a mere professor of comparative religion in a New Delhi university, answer our cry for help? Will Jain fight bare-chested and naked, his spirit resolved to save the masses shackled by old-order ordinances and false promises? What is Jain's answer? How will he bridge the philosophical divide that separates religions and fosters strife?

Who will end the present state of propaganda-blitzed limbo—the scientist, the philosopher, or the new prophet? Will the Age of Reason be followed by the Age of Truth or the Fourth World?

I write this book with immeasurable hope. What happened on the night of August 29, in the sky over the grounds surrounding a mosque in New Delhi, may liberate us all. Hope: more than a dream, hope is the diving board of action. I write with my soul at the tip of my fingers.

Gandharva raja

The Last Day of Ramadan

Nimbus

He, the first origin of this creation, whether he formed it all or did not form it, whose eye controls this world in highest heaven, he verily knows it, or perhaps he knows not. [Vedic Hymn]

It was several years after Osama bin Laden was killed. There was a perception among many that Osama's message had died with him. There were whispers that a holy man had arisen and that he was to deliver a new and different message. In anticipation of this message, a large crowd gathered around New Delhi's Jama Masjid. Men and women came in droves in response to distributed leaflets and news blogs on social media that he was to deliver his message tonight.

The masjid façade was ablaze with a million megawatts of light, and the surrounding city looked dim and dark in contrast. People overflowed from the mosque onto the grounds below. Women were allowed to pass and gather in the square till the quadrangle was filled with people and not one more could be squeezed in. We had gone in early and found a place on the rampart that surrounded the square. Considering the intensity of its anticipation, the crowd was unusually quiet and disciplined. Policemen guided the people with little coercion to form rows around the mosque. The crowd, mesmerized by the expectation of a great happening, waited patiently, from time to time looking at the sky above for a sign or an omen.

Orange and blue flames leapt upward from the large fire that burnt in the center of the quadrangle. People continued to gather in enlarging circles around the mosque as darkness snail-paced over the landscape and the sun leaned to the west and was lost in the belly of the night.

Ramadan ended this day with the appearance of the new moon—a silver talisman against the dark sky. The Prophet received the *Koran* from heaven during the holy month of Ramadan. Many in the crowd had come to these grounds the night before—Laylat alQadr, the Night of Power. Tonight was different. The crowd around Jama Masjid was larger. The air was heavy. Many thousand zealous eyes searched the sky with fervent anticipation.

A wisp of gray cloud hung from the crescent moon like a rope. The sun had set an hour ago. To the northeast, lights outlined the brick walls of the fort against the opaque night. From where we sat on the rampart, we saw a cone of light rise from the ground near the fort. At first indistinct, the distant roar of the helicopter strengthened as it approached the gathered crowd. The precisely timed lights on the fuselage blinked threateningly. The cone of light from the underbelly of the craft drew a wider, brighter circle as it approached the mosque, stepping over houses and shrubs. The crowd had turned to look in the direction of the approaching helicopter. It was now less than half a mile away.

Yuri, standing next to me, yelled into my ears, "Jain is in that helicopter, Gora! He has to be! He said, 'Look for me in the sky.' This is what he meant." A million eyes fixed on its path, the helicopter came within a few hundred yards of the mosque. I instinctively glanced back toward the inner sanctum of the masjid. I spotted the man in the black kaftan with the blue and white scarf around his head. He held a weapon in his hand, or so it seemed from this distance. He was in the far corner of the mosque quadrangle fifty to sixty feet from us. The figure was indistinct, but I was certain who it was. I pointed him out to Yuri. In the light of the flames, he flickered on and off like the changing pattern within a kaleidoscope. It was he—the man in my pocket Nikon: Syed Musa, the Egyptian ...

It was days after the happenings on that last day of Ramadan, the night of August 29, that I found the following script neatly folded and placed in the middle of a diary. The diary itself had no writings in it. It was blank except for the words inscribed on the first page in Professor Jain's own hand: "Kabir H. Jain." Hiding the diary from view was a copy of *The Passages*, which Jain kept on his bedside table. Yuri, Farooq, Milli, and I have read the writing on that folded sheet of paper a million times since.

The sun will set in a few hours. I will not see it rise again.

For the cause that helps the planet, and all that share the earth's bounty, the sacrifice I make will enrich my life and that of those who follow me.

God is merciful; God is compassionate—he who kills his child is cast from his compassion. I am one of God's trillion children. I share the bounty of his planet with his many children.

The highest of men—the ideal being—is molded in the cast

of God. He will be ill at ease on this earth.

I am the better fit for this world on which the sun shines and the clouds cast many shadows. Will I be dutiful in the eyes of God? He who does his duty perfectly is the perfect man. Have I been the perfect man?

The perfect man does what is good for this world where light and shadow play foolish games with one another. Ego is the eyelid's wink teasing wisdom. Too, ego is the foot-pedal of action. The perfect man is wisdom in action—all hurdles disappear before him.

A Day to Remember, A Day to Forget

Deep within them I will plant my law, writing it on their hearts. [Moses]

It was a day to remember, a day to forget; a day when life struggled to breathe through death's chokehold and survived; a day when death was diminished in the knowledge that it was he who was transient, and life that is eternal. It was a day to mourn, a day to rejoice. It was the night when the sky shone brighter than day, and succeeding days brighter than thirty million years ago when God created earth and flooded it with light. It was as if a searchlight on Mount Everest had spread light through the shadows of the universe so women, men, and children could walk into the gloomiest nook and cavern and not be afraid.

Seven years have passed since that night of August 29. As I sat on the chair by the window of our flat in the Daria Ganj section of New Delhi looking out at the mosque hazily outlined in the distance, Milli stood behind me, her hand resting gently on my shoulder. Milli and I chose this flat to live in after we got married four years ago. Each day we relived that night. The view of the mosque from our living room window kept alive the recollection of that day, distinct as the creases on my palms. Neither time nor distance had erased a word, a sound, a prayer, or a moan.

Seven years had not aged Milli. She looked beautiful in her white sari, its red border the exact same color as the vermillion dot on her forehead. On this August anniversary, she wore white.

It was after five in the afternoon. An hour later Yuri knocked on the door of our flat. He wore a red bandana around his forehead. Bending conspicuously as he came through the door, he said, "Lift the doorframe two inches, Gora. I am afraid I am going to hit my head against it one day."

Then he kissed Milli on the cheek. "There is no woman in Russia as pretty as you."

He placed his hands around my neck and pretended to choke me as he did each year on the anniversary day.

I reminded him, "We are now lecturers at the university, not the students we were seven years ago."

"Humbug," he said before he sat on the sofa chair in front of the television, his long legs stretched as far as they could reach. He turned on the TV and seconds later turned it off.

"Even Russia has better shows."

Yuri went to Russia once a year. He is fond of his mother. His father died before he came to Delhi eleven years ago. As he left for the airport each year to board the plane to Moscow, Yuri threatened that he might not return to India. But he came back. He taught anthropology at the university. Students packed his classes. The girls doted on him; to them he was a rock star.

"You look slim, Gora. Jogging is doing you good. Aha! You are growing your hair longer—makes you look like a poet. Was that Milli's suggestion? Shouldn't he have a beard too, Milli? I have never met a clean-shaven poet except Gora. A moustache would make his long nose look shorter."

"I don't have a long nose. I have long legs," I protested.

Milli smiled. "He is not just a poet. A lecturer in English lit has to look the part. The beard is out."

An hour later, at dusk, Farooq pounded on the door. He was always late and always in a hurry. "I can't keep up," he said. On another day he would have yelled, "Give me a cup of tea, Milli! I am dying of hunger." He would yank open the fridge, take out all that he liked, heap it on a plate, and spoon-feed himself before he took time out to say, "I hope you did not mind, Milli."

If Yuri poked fun at his ravenous appetite, he would reply, "Arrey baba [Okay, mister], I am emulating a Russian."

On this day of remembrance, he came in as the lamps in the sky were being turned on. He apologized for being late. He spoke little that evening. He shook my hand, then Yuri's.

He turned to Milli and said, "Namaste, bahan [Greeting, sister]. How are you?" He was so polite that I smiled. Yuri threw a mock punch at him. Farooq sat quietly at the edge of the sofa, his lean frame bent over his brown arms, his fingers interlocked. In spite of his food craze, he has remained slender. He works out at the gym.

Farooq pulled out a white hankie from his hip pocket and dabbed the corners of his eyes. Milli walked over and sat beside him.

"It has been seven years," he said. "I can't get over it. It happened yesterday."

I thought of Farooq as a rainbow; his emotions had as many colors as his finely embroidered shirts. He wore a thin moustache. He was handsome. Unlike me, Farooq was always impeccably dressed. Tonight his open vest was light blue and had brass buttons. Predictably, I wore a pair of khaki trousers and a black cotton shirt. I did not look like a poet.

That evening Sohaila came in behind Farooq. She sat beside him. Her delicate fingers rested in the comfort of Farooq's lap. She was his shadow. She was three inches shorter than Farooq, her complexion a shade darker than his. She nodded at each of us. She smiled, and her bright, white teeth lit up the room. She did not cover her head with a blue scarf that night. Her black hair flowed over the wheatish glow of her skin.

Before we asked, she announced, "I am ready for the evening."

As the sun began to set, we took our position on four square mats on the floor, our backs to a brass oil lamp placed in the center of the room. Sohaila stood by the window and observed our ritual. Yuri, Milli, Farooq, and I prayed silently for a few minutes, each remembering that twenty-ninth day in August—each in our own individual way—meditating on our unique emotions and memories of that night.

Milli had orchestrated the details of the ritual that we followed elaborately each year on this anniversary. Though Sohaila had kept her Muslim faith, she never missed being at our ritual. Too, she arranged and moderated the convention that followed our rituals. She had done so each year, willingly and graciously.

After the silent prayers, I rang the tiny bell that sat next to the oil lamp—four times. On the fourth ring, we turned to face the steady blue and orange flame of the lamp, and each other. Together we recited Diderot's prayer and then the prayer given to us by Jain. After the reading, we reached out, held hands, and meditated.

When the ritual ended, Milli placed the lamp on a pedestal near the window. The flame flickered in the gentle, warm breeze that beckoned the window and threw shadows on the walls—intricate, intriguing, and playful. Minutes later, darkness crept in through the window and made the lamp ever brighter.

After our private rituals were over, we headed down to the Assembly Hall, also located in the Daria Ganj section of the city and not far from the masjid. The hall, a one-story rectangular structure with pillars at the corners, had a rounded dome roof. Inside, the meeting hall occupied most of the built space with a wide podium up front and pew-style seating arranged as in a church. There were four small prayer rooms, one at each corner. A medium-sized bell hung from the ceiling of each prayer room such that there was a bell hanging—one each from the north, south, east, and west side of the building. The walls were white. On the wall behind the bell, Jain's prayer was inscribed in each prayer room. The mosaic floor was bare. A lamp burned on a pedestal near the inscribed wall in each prayer room. Nothing else was permitted in the prayer rooms where the men and women came to pray in silence.

People of various faiths and from all walks of life—professors, housewives, students, doctors, taxi drivers, seamstresses, gardeners, coolies, lawyers, preachers, and nurses—contributed to erect this hall where a meeting was held each year on the twenty-ninth of August. It was completed three years ago. A simple bronze plaque with Jain's likeness, embedded in the front exterior wall to the right of the front door, was inscribed with the date of the happening. To the left of the door, a large bronze bell was mounted on an eight-sided pedestal.

Sohaila had left copies of Jain's prayer inside. As people poured in, they collected a sheet and took their places in the pew. After Sohaila introduced the evening's events, various people, including a professor from JNU and a mullah from the mosque, gave speeches. Sohaila had begun, "He gave his life to liberate women like me."

"Why just women? He liberated us all," echoed the clergy.

Another said, "He saved the world from another war."

"Did Muhammad really appear before him?" someone asked.

When the night ended, people hugged each other as they walked out of the Assembly Hall door. I embraced Farooq, Sohaila, and Yuri. I saw a teardrop on Milli's cheek. Yuri had his hands deep in his pockets. Farooq held Sohaila's hands.

Those who had been at the masjid seven years earlier recalled the events of that night: the crowds around the mosque, the burning fire in the quadrangle, and the revelation.

We heard one say with conviction, "Indeed he was an avatar, a deity."

Another said, "He is a prophet."

The Heist

Do not store for yourselves treasures on earth ... For where your treasure is your heart is also. [Jesus: Sermon on the Mount]

The year Milli turned sixteen, her maternal grandfather who lived in Baltimore in the Fell's Point section of town, suffered a stroke that left him with severe weakness in the right arm and leg. His speech impaired, only Pamela's mother understood his blurred phrases. Milli's mother Pamela, a nurse at Johns Hopkins, had married Milli's father while he was training as a heart surgeon at the same hospital. The week after he completed his training, Milli's father boarded a plane to Delhi with his Caucasian wife where the couple settled in his ancestral home. Milli's parents had been to America several times in the eighteen years since they left Baltimore. After Milli was two, "Let's hop on a plane," Pamela would urge the surgeon. He would happily oblige. To him, traveling to Baltimore was a pilgrimage. The idol-worshipper would once again lay his eyes on the revered past. "To Osler," he would announce, lifting his glass high.

A month after her father had suffered the stroke, Milli's mother boarded the flight to Baltimore alone. She carried more baggage than usual. She stayed with her parents and lent her mother a helping hand. She was a nurse once again and cared for her father as she would a patient assigned to her care. She turned him in bed, sat him on a bedside rocker, elevated his feet on a pillow, and began to teach him how to speak again. "Papa, soon you will be up and walking with a cane."

A month later she let Milli and her father know that she planned to stay in Baltimore a while longer.

As her mother's next birthday approached, Milli shared a plan with us. She had her heart set on an exotic gift: a pendant, infinitely classic, enduringly beautiful—something very Mogul. "Will you accompany me this Sunday morning?" she asked.

Of course we would go—Yuri to satisfy his curiosity, I because I was in love, and Farooq Shahjehan because he was the perfect escort who knew the alleys and shops where stolen goods were sold. We would scour the section of Old Delhi where unusual objects were sold at fire-sale prices. Being from that section of town, Farooq could bargain with the shrewdest shopkeeper at heart's length. A spectacular heist would confer bragging rights to Farooq and bring a smile to Milli's face. Milli's smile could win over the entire city.

On the appointed Sunday morning in September, Yuri, Farooq, and I rang the doorbell at Milli's father's South Delhi villa. The sun diffused its pleasant warmth through the heavy fog caught between rows of sisal trees along the side wall of the villa compound. The quiet neighborhood had begun to stir. Drivers attended their employers' cars in the driveways, a bucket of water in hand and polishing and waxing the hood and chrome with vigor. A few ferrywallahs set out with baskets of fruits and vegetables on their head, trumpeting their produce in a sonorous staccato: "Aloo, gobi, baigan [potato, cabbage, eggplants]." After we had waited a full five minutes on the verandah in front of the house, a servant opened the door. He asked us if we would prefer to wait outside since Milli would be down "in no time." So we did not feel slighted, he left the door ajar. Minutes later, a woman with a light blue hijab, wearing a knee-length black abaya and a white salwar, walked past us through the open door without saying a word. A niqab of fine lace veiled her face. A new worker or a friend of Milli's, we guessed. Once out of the front gate, the woman turned around, leaned coquettishly against the black sedan parked out front, waved at us, and with mock displeasure called out, "You guys coming, or will you continue to gawk?" It was Milli. My heart sank. Before I could open my heart to her, the world would fall in love with Milli.

Milli was driving. She did not heed her chauffer's protests. On Farooq's advice, she parked the car four blocks away from our destination: the thief's market. It would be discreet to walk the rest of the way since a brightly polished long black sedan parked in front of the shop would betray any bargaining advantage we purportedly possessed.

Dimly lit shops lined the narrow lane on both sides. Glass cases displayed jewels, necklaces, statues of deities, and clothing laced with silver and gold threads. Statuettes of Ganesha and Krishna outnumbered all others. One shop's display was not outwardly different from the next. After walking through several lanes, Milli decided on a shop deep in the heart of Kinari Bazaar. "Gota Jewelers," the signboard announced in Hindi and Urdu. The crowd was thick around it. It was Milli's hunch that indeed the loot was there.

"We are going to take back the Kohinoor—avenge the sacking of the Somnath Temple. I will wring the neck of the barbarian Ghazni." I threw my verbal jab at Farooq.

"Don't start a riot, Gora," Yuri warned as we entered the shop.

"He who taketh may give back; he who was taken will back off," Farooq fought back.

"Don't start anything, you two. We have a mission," Milli pleaded through her burqa.

"Farooq was indoctrinated into bhajans at an impressionable age. There will be no riots," I assured her.

Inside the shop, Yuri pursued the topic.

"If I could lay my hand on one large ruby from the idol's belly, I would buy a villa like Milli's and marry your sister, Gora."

Far from being annoyed, I was relieved. One down. At least Yuri had not set his target on Milli. He would have been a formidable opponent. The idle conversation had diverted my attention from Milli. She was rummaging through the loot somewhere in the back of the shop. I picked up a copy of Kahlil Gibran's The Prophet, illustrated with his own mystical drawings. I was reading "to the bee a flower is a fountain of life, and to the flower the bee is a messenger of love, and to both bee and flower, the giving and receiving of pleasure is a need and an ecstasy," when I realized that Farooq and Yuri were no longer in the store. And Milli, who should have been rummaging through the heist, had backed off to the entrance door and was absorbed in the crowd gathering in front of Jari Jewelers, a shop in the near corner on the opposite side of the street from Gota Jewelers.

A scuffle was beginning. A curious crowd was gathering

around the melee. Yuri, with his long steps, was halfway there and Farooq was close behind him. I snapped the booklet shut, caught up with Milli at the entrance door, and pulled her along across the street, keeping a safe distance from the maelstrom. I had to protect her.

At the epicenter of the storm was a boy of about fourteen. His long tasseled fez was tilted precariously from being pushed and shoved. The owner of Jari Jewelers held the young boy by the collar with his left hand and ominously shook his right clenched fist close to the boy's face, threatening a first strike. He alleged loudly that the boy had stolen a gem from the head of a statue of Krishna. The shopkeeper's clerk swore he had seen the boy leave just as he discovered that the precious jewel was missing.

The boy pleaded innocence: "Search me. I have nothing."

The shopkeeper urged the crowd to take the law in their own hand and bestow just punishment on the jewel thief. "The police do nothing to stop thieves and robbers."

The clerk was emphatic. "The police and thieves are together. We must punish the boy right here and now."

The antiauthoritarian rhetoric aroused the crowd. The shopkeeper and his clerk were about to deal the young boy his due, when a tall man wearing an open kurta over jeans forced his way through the crowd and pulled the boy behind him.

The man shouted to the crowd, "No one lay a finger on this boy. No one can be punished till he is found to be guilty."

The man assured the crowd that he would see to it that the boy was interrogated at the police station. The jeweler proclaimed to the crowd that the intruder was likely the master thief in cahoots with his apprentice. The clerk added that the intruder deserved a beating as much as the boy did. The intruder was not cowed. He pushed his way out of the crowd to a Jeep parked near the street corner, his arm around the teenager's shoulders.

As he pulled away from the crowd, the intruder shouted to the shopkeeper, "Come to the police station. I will meet you there. You can file charges."

He offered the shopkeeper's clerk a ride in the Jeep.

The clerk refused. "It is useless. Everything is fixed."

"Whatever you find disagreeable, you must try to change." The intruder's voice was calm and deliberate.

The crowd was divided. Many announced their support for the jeweler. Another section of the crowd, embracing the man as a savior, shouted, "Jitey Raho, may you live long." A few young kids ran after the Jeep.

We pulled back from the crowd as it began to disperse. I realized then that the book The Prophet was in my hand. Parting her niqab, Milli tugged at my shirt. She looked toward the Jeep and sighed. "He is my hero." My heart sank to a new low. I was there. I had the opportunity. I could have been Milli's hero.

Milli walked ahead. A few steps later, she turned around. "Did you pay for the book, Gora?"

The Last Day of Ramadan

Farooq Shahjehan

In the alterations of night and day; in the water which God sends down from the sky and with which He revives the earth after its death ... in the clouds that are driven between sky and earth: surely in these there are signs for rational men. [Koran 2:164]

I came to know Farooq Shahjehan when I was growing up in South Delhi. While I trudged to school, did my homework, and joined the family in the courtyard for the mandatory evening bhajan [devotional singing to the beat of clapping and cymbals], Farooq was flying kites and spinning tops on the pavements of Old Delhi. Lest someone mistakenly perceive that I spent my childhood in Dickensian drudgery under the low-hung eyeglasses of an evil, bullying uncle, let me dispel all doubts before I introduce Farooq.

I confess that as a child I preferred reading to playing cricket or soccer. Not that I did not enjoy the company of other kids in the neighborhood. I did. I roamed the by-lanes and climbed trees in search of the ripe guava. But to me, ducking compulsory late-afternoon school sports to read Tagore's Gora, Saratbabu's Srikanta, or Shakespeare's Romeo and Juliet was far more enthralling than a cricket follow-on. Tree branches make the best seats in the house.

Presence at the evening bhajan was not coerced but expected of us. For my part, I would never miss it. It was the best part of my life as a child. Before evening lengthened its shadow and cast us in darkness, the preparation began with mother spreading a large rug on the courtyard floor. My sister, four years my elder, would then light the lamps at the four corners of the open space before she sat down next to Father. My two uncles, my father's younger brothers, took their respective places on the carpet when they returned from work. Father sat up front near the altar of Shiva-Parvati. His white dhoti and kurta contrasted with my sister's yellow sari till the sun went down and the colors merged. After the wicker-lamp at the altar was lit, Father would raise his arms as a sign for Mother to blow on the conch shell. Then the cymbals clashed spiritedly and the singing began. The keeper of the cymbals, my brother, older by three years, and I sat behind Father.

Om! Jaya Jagadisha Harey. Om! Praise the Almighty God.
Om! Jaya Jagadisha Harey. Om! Praise the Almighty God.
Bhaktajanakay sankata Any foreboding in the faithful
kshanmein doora karey. is vanished instantly by You.

I first met Farooq on one such evening. The singing had begun, with my father leading the chorus. Halfway through the ritual for the evening, my brother thrust his elbow into my ribs, clashing the cymbal an extra decibel higher.

"There is someone at the front door. Go open it." Convinced by a second jab, I rose to obey his command, elevating my melody to a higher pitch lest Father misinterpret my departure as evidence of my lack of devotion.

"Tana, mana, dhana saab tera [body, mind and possessions are all Yours]."

"My father, Latif Mian, sent me to deliver these clothes. My name is Farooq Shahjehan. Here are three shirts and four blouses. Please count them. My father said that I should tell you that the total cost is nine hundred and seven rupees. He will be pleased if you pay now as he has to buy cloth from the market tomorrow."

I asked Farooq to come in, happy that he was about my age. My family was still immersed in devotional singing. I pointed to a space on the carpet. He hesitated at first and then sat on the steps close by.

Cymbals marked the end of that evening's event with a clang. Mother blew thrice on the conch shell, long and hard. She remarked that Latif, the tailor, had a good-looking son. "Look how fair he is! He will be taller than Latif Mian when he grows up."

At Father's insistence, Farooq swallowed two biscuits with a cup of milk. He was given the sum of nine hundred and seven rupees and sent on his way with the caution to be extremely careful. Evening cloaks the wicked. The streets were not safe for a young boy carrying such a large sum of money.

After he left, mother told me that I may have offended Farooq by asking him to sit on a Hindu prayer rug. Latif Mian was an ardent Muslim, though of course a very decent man.

Yuri

He who sees all beings in his own self and his own self in all beings,
does not suffer from any repulsion by that experience.
[Isa Upanishad]

Yuri did not consider himself a scholar. A scholar is more than a pocket PDA.

A scholar can connect the dots and come up with a vision. Yuri was the master visionary. He could see dots that no one else saw and come up with a picture. There was little doubt in my mind that Yuri was a scholar. An exchange student to JNU from Moscow, he was six foot one, standing a good three inches over me and at least three inches wider at the shoulders. The strong features on his clean-shaven face made him attractive if not outright handsome. He had a habit of keeping his hands deep in his trouser pockets when he was walking with his brisk long steps and his signature brown suede shoes.

I was polishing my black leather shoes when Yuri had walked into the dorm room that I shared with Farooq.

"Why bother?" Yuri said. "Delhi has more dust than those bristles can clean." He shook my hands as he said fluently in Hindi, "Mera naam Yuri. Mein Russian hoon. Mein do darbaja pichey hoon. I am Yuri. I am from Russia. I am two doors down."

Yeltsin must have looked like Yuri when young, I thought. Before I could say to him, "I am Gora and I am glad to meet you," Farooq was introducing himself.

"As-salaam alaikum. I am Farooq. I live with this heathen."

"Nice," Yuri replied, pointing to Farooq's chin.

This was my first month at Jawaharlal Nehru University. After our first meeting at the evening prayer, I had seen Farooq on several other occasions when he came to deliver newly sewn clothes to our home. Now Farooq was a slim handsome youth with a thin mustache and a finely pointed goatee. He was not as tall as my mother had predicted on my first meeting with Farooq. He was a good two inches shorter than me. I was five eleven. This was our first encounter with Yuri. Henceforth we spent much of our spare time together. Yuri was fun to be with, always energized and looking for something to do. Farooq had his ups and downs. He was moody. Still, we got along well.

Typical of a Sunday in those carefree early days of college life, Yuri, Farooq, and I left our stuffy dorms and headed to the market section of Delhi not far from JNU. The morning air was pleasant and the shops not overcrowded. We walked aimlessly, Yuri with a red bandana around his golden brown hair, Farooq with his signature blue embroidered vest over a white shirt, and I in my usual khaki trouser and black polo. With no particular shopping list in hand, we entered a shop in the outskirts of Delhi not far from the university.

As we entered the shop, a painting that hung on the back wall caught our eyes instantly. It was unlike the other paintings that clung to the walls and unlike the others stacked in piles behind the shop-counter. I call the gallery a shop because, besides the paintings, etchings, and a few statuettes, a myriad other sundry objects were on display. Papier-mâché dolls from Kashmir, plastic ones made in Agra, packaged Darjeeling tea, small black tins marked Nestlé's Instant Coffee and stacks of Mysore Sandalwood Soap were flung together with eclectic abandon much like the urban sprawl of outer Delhi.

The name on the tag attached to the painting was Russian.

"Reminds me of Boris Pasternak," Yuri said as he pointed to the painting. My eyes were already on it. Four wooden chairs placed near the corners of the canvas formed an asymmetric quadrangle. The frothy sea-line cut across the legs of two chairs on the foreground of the canvas. The gaunt jester sat bare-bodied on a rock within the quadrangle. Behind him the sun was mellow. A bemused smile pursed its lips around the stem of a two-headed flute. Seadeep blue-gray eyes bore the sorrow of dark clouds. The eyes lingered on the notes as they floated out of the flute and dropped back into the sea, soaked in brine, spray, and mist.

"You wish to change the world, Gora? You must give up poetry. Poetry is the futile attempt of our drowning world to stay afloat, paddling with soft iambic pentameters to cross a thousand feet against all odds, to scan the shore and be saved. Poetry is gunned by the artillery of empty shells. A poet is a mariner with an albatross around his neck."

"A few mixed metaphors there." Yuri had answered his own question.

I smiled. I was still capturing the details of the painting. If a painted scene can captivate the heart, poetry surely can hold sway over the mind. Modern poetry is flat when it is contrived; stale because the words are cliché. I was not going to involve Yuri in an intellectual debate at that moment. He was fully charged.

"Remember, Gora, art is long, life is short, and the memory of Stalin even shorter. How many remember one detail of Stalin beyond that he killed millions? Pasternak made 'the whole world weep at the beauty' of Russia. No one can forget Zhivago's Russia: death and passion intertwined in the embrace of love, the last embrace of a woman the lover will never set eyes on again."

Yuri paused. Both Farooq and I remained silent. We could see the thin lips on Yuri's clean-shaven face quiver.

"Zhivago could not save Russia any more than Stalin."

At the end of the plaintive concession, Yuri threw me a challenge. "If Gora can create a poem on this painting in the next three minutes, I will acknowledge that he, contrary to Aristotle's opinion, is not merely a poet but an upcoming do-gooder."

Farooq was examining an ivory embossed dagger-sheath. "This is hand-carved in Rajasthan, Yuri," he said. Then he pointed the dagger toward me and mocked, "And if you fail, I will do the poet in."

The man behind the sales counter had obviously followed our conversation with participatory curiosity. He handed me a pad and a pencil. He too was daring me. I took a deep breath. I closed my eyes. The lines of the drawing—the painting were vividly etched on my mind. The words that rippled over my tongue were the waves rolling over the sand and breaking into bubbles and froth in a changing pattern based on a timeless, complex, and eternal rhythm. I began to write.

Minutes later, I think it was more than three, looking around and assuring myself that there were only four people in the gallery, I reeled off recklessly:

Two-headed Musician

on whose breast the sky meets earth—
God of Sea,
you who churn the salt of life,
I die in your arms.
Carry me to a rival shore
unseen below the swell.
Let my flesh give life to fish and snail.
On the grip of tentacles
let me scale the contrary shore.
Do not grieve.
I will arise.

The salesman clapped.

Yuri gave me a Russian bear hug. Then he said, "Say it with more passion, Gora. Smile when you speak of death. Bring tears to your words, but not your eyes—you will be a great poet. You will win the Nobel Prize."

Farooq, who after he was done with appreciating the ivory dagger sheath had been flipping through stacks of painted canvas, gestured that his vote too was cast in my ballot box.

We browsed around the store a while longer, curious how a genuine work of Russian contemporary art found its way to the outskirts of Delhi.

I asked the shopkeeper if he knew how the painting was acquired. He did not know. He was only a clerk. The owner would be in the next day. Would I come and meet him? Mr. Pande would have the answer and perhaps my foreigner friend would buy the painting from him.

Yuri overheard him. "If I ever make a living on cultural anthropology, I will be back to buy the painting," he said with feigned despair.

Insecurity of Poetry

Women shall with justice have rights similar to those exercised against them, although men have a status above women. God is mighty and wise. [Koran 2:228, 229]

On my first day of classes at JNU, I noticed the pretty girl in pink sari and blue blouse sitting two benches to the front and to the right of me. I remember little of what was said in the introductory session. I simply could not take my eyes off the girl in the pink and blue. During the course of the hour she had noticed this. She smiled as she turned her face away. It took me a week to introduce myself to Milli.

Milli's father came from an old line of doctors. Her grandfather had been a professor of medicine at Delhi University. She remembered him vaguely as a kindly man in a light gray suit and a black tie, with white hair and a playful smile. A black stethoscope hung around his neck when he came back from work late in the evening. He would clean the earpiece and the bell-diaphragm with spirit and let Milli listen to his heart with it. "Lub-doob, Lub-doob," Milli would laugh. Milli was seven when he died in his sleep. Milli's father, the heart surgeon, was tall and statuesque with broad shoulders and long legs. Unlike his own father, he was intense. Two years after the heart surgeon and nurse Pamela appeared before a judge in Baltimore, exchanged vows, and became man and wife, Milli was born. Milli was now a student at the university.

Three years passed since her mother had left for Baltimore to care for her elderly parents. The heart surgeon visited Maryland often. "Gives me a chance to attend the conference at Hopkins," he would announce apologetically as he packed his suitcase.

"Johns Hopkins fell in love with his cousin Elizabeth Hopkins. His uncle did not permit them to marry. Quaker rules, Milli. Neither ever married."

Milli accompanied him on some of these visits. Each time the doctor asked Pamela to come back to Delhi, she would kiss her husband on his cheeks and say "Someday soon, love." When Milli hugged her mother fiercely and cried, "I miss you, Mommy," Pamela would stroke her cheeks and say, "Do you know how much I miss you?"

This year, her first at Jawaharlal Nehru University, Milli stayed behind in Delhi. Father went alone. "Only for a week, Milli!"

During that first year at JNU, I sought out Milli at every break the busy college routine presented to me. If I saw her at the cafeteria, I bought her a cup of coffee. At the library, I sat at her table and turned the pages of a book absorbing nothing, my mind totally emptied by the thought of Milli. On some Sundays, I invited her to the movies. She was equally fond of Hollywood and indigenous fare. Often Yuri and Farooq joined us at the cafeteria or the movie. As the year progressed, the four of us banded together as though we had known each other growing up as children from a familiar neighborhood.

Whether in salwar-kameez, sari, or Western jeans and top, Milli stood out in any crowd. Half the young men at college fell in love with Milli the instant they saw her. The rest fell in love the moment she began to speak. With waves of black hair, thin curled lips, dark brown eyes, and wheat-flour complexion, Milli stood bare feet an inch below five and a half, an inch above with heels on.

One morning on our way to class, a few months after we had met Professor Jain in our second year at JNU, Milli and I were walking along the Jamun tree-lined lane that led to the library near the Center for Study of Law and Governance. We talked about sundry things, neither legal nor legislative. When we reached the bottom of the steps leading up to the library, the conversation turned to philosophy for no particular reason but that since meeting Jain it had been on my mind.

"I have been thinking about creation and the controversies that surround it," I blurted out.

Milli looked me in the eye. I felt a bio-probe pierce my retina and measure the height of my intellect and the depth of my soul. This was Milli's way. Milli was hard candy.

"Stayed up all night and read the *Chandogya Upanishad*, Gora? You are better off with *God of Little Things* and *Harry Potter and the Prisoner of Azkaban*, you know."

Taunting her with a pavonine strut, I replied, "School girl stuff, Milli. Remember we stand on the steps of JNU." Then as an afterthought, I added, "You know Milli, all religious texts need to be revised. Even the Hindu texts, the *Vedas*, need to be reexamined."

"Oh! Really?" Milli raised her eyebrows one regal notch higher. I was being challenged. This was my chance. Positive vibes stirred my heart. I pulled out a multifolded piece of paper from my hip pocket. Slowly I unfolded it, gauging Milli's reaction as I did so. "Listen with reverence. For this is Brahma":

The atom and the whole—I am the circle that holds
life and death hereafter, the doleful song of the soul.
I am what you make of me—the constant and the change,
I am the circle that holds—stars revolve within me.

I paused. With a silent gesture, Milli encouraged me to continue. I felt my heart skip a beat.

Behind the pupil of your eye, my image unseen—
I am the Reason—I am the circle that holds.
I am the circle that holds—the expanding arc of the galaxy,
all words written, every story told.

Milli turned and walked up the steps of the building. I chastised myself for the stupid attempt to win a girl's heart with dry and dreary lines on deity. Why galaxy, why not something more Anglo-Saxon? I was heartbroken. I was destined to sing bhajans on my wedding night, I scolded myself.

Life can turn on a girl's heel. There was Milli running down the steps.

"That was lovely, Gora. Really!"

She gave me a gentle hug. I felt her small breasts against my chest.

I was in love. I would never recover.

Kabir H. Jain

Not by refraining from action does one achieve renunciation—
the energies that drive nature, drive the mind to action
... [Bhagavad-Gita]

Toward the end of our first year at JNU, it became our practice to spend Saturday evenings at the Rajah Fountain and Bar. The café/bar was within easy reach of our campus and not far from Rockland Inn in Greater Kailash. Farooq, Yuri, and I rarely missed the chance for small talk over sandwiches and beer from the tap. Milli often made the fourth. "A snazzy dig," she had exclaimed on her first visit to the Rajah, pointing to the red velvet wall covering and the comfortable black leather lined chairs.

In the cozy coolness of the joint, we compared class notes, disparaged the current state of the world, and made lighthearted fun of each other. Consuming a few glasses of beer and a dozen sandwiches each week had established us as regulars at the Rajah.

One evening at the Rajah Fountain, Yuri was more upbeat than his usual emphatic demeanor. Finding him gung-ho, I suggested that we toast Russia with a round of vodka. To my surprise, Yuri said no. Rather emphatically. I would have ignored the nyet had he not at the same time grabbed my arm and gripped it hard and long. He was upset. But why? After he let go of my arm, I waited for an explanation. Yuri shook his head several times. Then he apologized. "Gora, I did not mean to hurt you."

We sat silently for a few minutes. Yuri had always thrown in tidbits of Russian lore and about his own life in the old country when we chatted leisurely in a café or on a stroll along one of Delhi streets. I tried to fathom from what Yuri had shared with us in the past what triggered his uncharacteristic vexation.

"My father lived in Gorky outside Moscow. During the war he met my mother in Czechoslovakia. After the war they got married. My father joined the Party and moved to Moscow. I was born in an eight-story apartment building. It was outside the Third Ring—Tretye Koltso. Our one-bedroom unit was small. My father was a husky Russian, tall and muscular. Remember Yeltsin? Father looked a lot like him. After a while, Father became disenchanted with the Party: being obedient, the fear, the hush-hush. He took to vodka. I was ten."

Yuri sipped on a glass of water before he continued.

"I remember Mother looking out of our fifth-floor window when it was time for Father to return after work. I remember seeing her rush down the stairs when she spotted him stagger into view. Once inside our small flat, Father would slump on a sofa. He was soon out like the light. I would look at Mother and feel sad. She would light a cigarette—exhausted after the effort of helping him up the stairs. I would turn to look at Father slouched on the couch oblivious to the pain he had caused. I felt angry. But as I lingered over his pitiful slump, my anger gave way to a strange kind of love for him.

In the next few months, my father lost a great deal of weight.

He had been as big as I am now. Father began to lose his health. His jawbones jutted like a bare knuckle. His ribs were arched and lined like the bird cage wire. He coughed all night. He became thinner. The doctor said he had TB. He was dead in a year. I was eleven. No vodka. Never, never, never."

Henceforth at the Rajah we stuck to lassi, cola, coffee, beer, and occasionally wine. We met at the Fountain every week and oftener if a happy event called for it and the purse permitted.

One college year was over and we were planning for the next. That Saturday Milli was not coming to the Rajah. She had a party to go to with her father. Farooq, Yuri, and I arrived at the Rajah early in the evening. We were assigned a table with four seats in the middle of the joint.

"Not a drop for you, Farooq. Good friends will preserve your Muslim orthodoxy," Yuri teased as he uncorked a bottle of red wine.

"Not even the froth of my Kingfisher," I hummed along.

"I don't know Shia from Sunni. I do know Saudis are Sunnis and they come to Mumbai to drink. I am Latif Mian's son and my father is a devout Muslim." Farooq poured himself a generous glass of wine during this verbal distraction. The cup overflowed. The red stain besmirched the white tablecloth.

"Blame the idol-worshipping infidel, Gora. I forfeited my claim to seven virgins in paradise the moment I sat in on his bhajan chant. Is it seven or ten?"

"Spilling costly vintage is sin in any religion. If Gora had not done you in, I would," Yuri threatened as he repossessed the bottle of wine. "Eleven hundred rupees is a lot of rubles for an exchange student at JNU."

The Last Day of Ramadan

Farooq lifted the glass with his left hand. "Soma, make me shine like fire. Make Yuri spill all his rubles. I too am broke. Get Gora so drunk that he cries out 'Allah Ho Akbar' thrice before he is thrown out of the bar." At this Yuri and I grabbed him by the neck and pretended to choke him. He made the sign of peace and we burst out laughing.

I let go of Farooq and was back in my chair when I overheard the man seated at the table behind ours speaking out.

"Allah is great. Does it matter if he is greater than Christ or Brahma? Does it really matter? So much is at stake."

The man seated at the table behind ours had spoken without turning his head. Alone at his table, eyes fixed on the open pages of a book, he sipped spring water from a glass held in the cup of his hands.

Annoyed by the stranger's eavesdropping, I mocked rudely, "Hare Krishna, Hare Ram."

The establishment—the black-shirted bartender, two white clad waiters, and the manager in a tight fitting navy blue suit—stared at me with glaring disapproval. I must have been loud. I felt a strong tug on my shirt. I sat down. It was Farooq.

"It is him," he whispered.

His glass of water in hand, the man from the next table came over to ours. "May I?" he asked as he sat down at our table—Milli's hero, in an open kurta and blue jeans. He was taller than he had appeared at the melee in Kinari Bazaar. I took a good look at him. He was well built, an inch or an inch and a half shy of six feet. Gently curled hair rolled onto his shoulders. His eyes were bright, eager to illuminate a dark universe. Images stored in the synapses of his brain scintillated in the light of his eyes.

I do not exaggerate. I have never seen eyes that were brighter.

"Jesus was a great storyteller," he said. "His life reads like a story. The parables! How delightful. Muhammad was a skilled leader—without fear, a sword in one hand, a scripture in the other. You talked of soma, the wine of the Vedic gods. The Vedas fell from the skies. Confucius is wisdom and Buddha doctrine. I am Jain."

There was an aura about Jain. He spoke clearly and with confidence. We took in every word that he spoke. We did not interrupt him.

After introducing himself as Jain, he paused. "I will teach comparative religion at JNU this academic year. I invite the three of you to attend my class."

Without any further expansion of this introduction, Milli's hero left the bar, leaving us stunned. I was bewildered. What if Milli too decided that taking a semester of world religion was a good idea!

The Liar

Believers, if an evil-doer brings you a piece of news inquire first into its truth, lest you should wrong others unwittingly and then regret your action. [Koran 49:6]

My newly acquired confidence would have endured had not the following incident occurred not too long after my coronation by the library steps. What jarred my moorings took place at the Rajah Fountain and Bar that very week. Yuri, Farooq, and I had decided to enroll for Jain's divine lecture series. It was Milli's suggestion that we meet with Jain before the classes began to get a personal preview of the courses. She would decide then if she too should register for the course.

"Let's ask Professor Jain," she said. "Worst case, he will decline. It will be nice if he says yes. He is quite charming."

Milli can be persuasive, though I missed the charm part. Yuri and I sought out Professor Jain at the university. We were hesitant—reluctant to offend him with the invitation. He said yes, indeed he was eager. I will do anything for Milli.

That Saturday evening, Farooq and I went in early to occupy a table at the Rajah. The place was noisy and packed to capacity. A dozen or so students queued outside the door, some audibly exhaling cigarette smoke while they stomped their feet and waited impatiently. This watering hole for students from nearby colleges served ice cream in tall glasses and beer and cold drinks from the tap. It could seat fifty in a squeeze. The menu hosted a brief selection of appetizers, kabobs, and sandwiches, a meager choice of the hard stuff, and a scant selection of wine. Still Rajah's was a classy cut, a notch above our station, considering that none of us except Milli were baked with the upper crust.

Milli came in a few minutes before Yuri. As the four of us waited for Jain, our discussion turned to religion and from there inevitably to terrorism. Farooq vociferously argued against neo-colonialism.

"Bush lost the battle and the war. Barak Hussein Obama is swaying like a poplar in the breeze."

Yuri too was skeptical. "You can't hide afterthoughts behind a banner. Call the saitan, a saitan! You are better off. The world is better off calling the devil a devil."

Milli sided with Yuri. "This political correctness is for the birds. I want to be nice to the next guy, but do I have to put ashes over my feelings and chant like a hypocrite?"

I was right. Milli is hard candy, I thought.

Farooq grimaced but said nothing in rebuttal.

I was undecided. "Something has to be done. I don't know if the new man in Washington can do it."

I knew it as soon as I said it! That was shilly-shally! Milli was on my mind. I wanted to pitch in but could not find the right words. I had struck too high a note with "Brahma"—anything I prepared to say since was bound to fall short. Desperate to erase any impression of indecisiveness I may have imparted to Milli by that last equivocation, I was about to cast my vote on open speech when Professor Jain walked in through the glass door. I decided magnanimity would surely impress a girl. I rushed to the door, escorted Jain to our table, and formally introduced him to Milli. Jain said, "Pranam" out of respect for a young lady.

Professor Jain took the chair we had kept for him. Once familiar with our topic, he voiced his opinion. His view was simple and to the point. "Nothing justifies an attack on civilians. No cause is good enough. It is a cowardly act and more of us should take an active role against it." Jain paused.

"The staunchest counterattack is to disrupt the thought process of the terrorist—make him uncertain about his flawed core. Undo the brainwashing!"

"How?" I asked.

Jain was about to elaborate when a melee broke out in the café. A young man at the table behind us was shaking the waiter, a boy I guess to be fifteen, by the collar. He accused the boy of lying. He claimed that he gave the waiter two hundred-rupee notes and two fifties to cover a bill of two hundred and seventy. The waiter had come back asking for more, saying that he received one hundred-rupee note and three fifties.

The young man shoved the waiter against a table declaring that he would pay "not one paisa more" but dole out in kind if he was further harassed by a young kid.

The waiter was scared. "If you don't pay, I will lose my job."

The young man was not mollified.

"The only thing you have learnt in life is to lie and steal," the young man yelled. He rushed at the waiter and launched a fierce punch at the young boy standing expectantly with his hand out for the extra money owed. Before the punch connected, Jain leapt to his feet and foiled the blow in midair. He placed himself between the accused and the accuser. The waiter shook with fear. The accuser straightened his shirt and prepared to return to his table. Jain took his wallet out.

"This should make up the balance. Please give the extra to the kid."

The manager vouched for the kid's honesty as he accepted a fifty-rupee note from Jain. Farooq nodded his approval of Jain. Milli's eyes were fixed on Jain. There was admiration in her eyes.

"If the boy can learn to lie, he can be taught to tell the truth. No one is born with a lie or a truth," he reminded the would-be boxer.

Quiet returned to the café.

Back at the table, I looked woefully at Milli.

The Origin...Greatness Is Its Own Guide

Then the Lord stretched his hand and touched my mouth.
And the Lord said to me, "See! I put my words in your mouth." [Jeremiah]

At the furtive end of the woeful glance, I heard Milli pop the question. "Where were you born, Professor Jain?" Calm had returned to the bar and we were seated again in our respective chairs.

As I sat at the table confounded by Milli's apparent fascination with Jain, I could not quash my own curiosity about this man whom unrelated circumstances had thrust upon our lives. I listened to Jain telling us that he was born to Shabana and Rahim Humayun, a Muslim couple in Ahmedabad, Gujarat. His father Humayun, a lecturer of Indian history at Ahmedabad College, was dead-set against religious orthodoxy. One of Humayun's closest friends was his next-door neighbor Professor Nikhil Jain, the chair of the history department at the college. Nikhil and his wife Maya, who were of the Hindu faith, were childless. They loved Shabana and Humayun's son Kabir as their own. Young Kabir, while he grew up as a child, was as much at home in his parents' house as at the neighbors'.

"We have no other children, Kabir, except you. Everything in this house is yours," Maya would frequently say while she prepared a dish of chapatti and curry for the ever hungry child.

Milli leaned forward on the table as Jain told us more about his childhood. In the backyard of the house of Nikhil and Maya, there was a small garden with mums, roses, scarlet-hued caladium, coleus with large green leaves with a dab of yellow in the middle, hibiscus with deep red flowers, and a banana tree—all commonly seen in the middle-class Indian home privileged to have a garden in the back of the house. The two men sat on easy chairs facing the garden, sipping lassi on balmy evenings, while the mothers gossiped in the kitchen. Young Kabir moved back and forth from the kitchen to the garden.

"I remember when I told them that my baba's [father's] face was long and Mr. Jain's was round, and that Nikhil Jain had more gray hairs than his baba, Nikhil would pout and make a sad face. I would put my arms around the professor's neck and say, 'Don't be hurt. You have a pretty face too.'"

For a moment Jain sat in silence. Sadness filled his eyes. What he said next was appalling. The year he turned seven, his parents, Rahim and Shabana Humayun, were out to see the rerun of an old movie called *Mughal-e-Azam*. It was an evening show. They left their young son with Professor and Maya Jain. Out of nowhere, communal riots broke out in Ahmedabad that night. A Muslim boy had harassed a Hindu girl, it was later alleged. Insanity gripped the section of town where the cinema hall was located. On their way back from the movie, Rahim and Shabana were dragged out of their car. Both were stabbed to death.

Farooq gripped his glass tightly with both hands. As Jain

went on with his story, we learnt that in time the madness cooled off. Jain stayed on in the house of Nikhil and Maya and, as the city returned to uneasy normalcy, Nikhil Jain adopted the son of his friend and neighbor—the professor was respected as a man of kindness and wisdom, and no one objected. Young Kabir Humayun assumed the name of Kabir H. Jain.

Maya Jain poured all her love onto young Kabir, rarely letting him out of her sight. The professor and his wife took the young boy out to the mall where cotton candy was sold, to the stall in the center of town where comic books were stacked. In spite of the doting love and ceaseless attention of his adoptive parents, there were days when young Jain was lost in deep, dark melancholy.

"One day I cried as I clutched the photo of my mother, Shabana. My mother Maya came over and hugged me and kissed me on my forehead."

"When I am grown up and strong, I will bring my mother back," Jain had said as he sobbed with his head buried in Maya's lap.

On another evening, young Jain stood in front of a photograph of Rahim and Shabana that the professor had hung in an elaborate frame in the room that the young boy slept in. Kabir held in his hands a bunch of flowers from the hibiscus bush that grew in the back garden of his new home. The young boy, then eight, was speaking to his dead father unaware that Nikhil Jain had walked in.

"I am so sad, Baba. Why did you not take me to the movie too? I will kill them all, Baba. When I grow up, I will kill them all."

Nikhil Jain had turned the boy around gently to face him. He had wiped the boy's tears with the tail of his shirt. Then he said, "When you grow up you will know love and hate. And you will choose the better of the two."

Jain repeated what his adoptive father had said twice.

As we listened to Jain, I imagined the child Jain waking up in the middle of the night gripped by fear and grief. I imagined Nikhil and Maya running to his side to comfort him. There was more to Jain's story.

As I had explained to Yuri after we returned to our dorm, devout Hindus considered the city of Ayodhya as one of the holiest. Rama, considered a deity by Hindus, was said to have been born there. A Rama temple had been built in the city many years ago. Centuries later, in 1527, the first Mughal emperor, Babar, invaded India. Babar's general, Mir Baqi, allegedly demolished the Rama temple and upon the site built the three-domed Babri Mosque, named after the Emperor Babar. A national debate about the myth and facts surrounding the Rama temple and Babri Masjid, which both Hindus and Muslims claimed as their own, had piqued the interest of the history department which Professor Nikhil Jain chaired.

After a discovery trip to Ayodhya, several members of the department, including Nikhil Jain, boarded a train to return to Ahmedabad. At the predominantly Muslim town of Godhra, the train was attacked by a mob. As stones smashed the windows, the passengers bolted the compartment doors. The train began to pull out of the station, but before it could roll out to safety someone pulled the alarm chain and the train came to a screeching halt. Agonizing minutes later, the train was ablaze in the flame of passion and bigotry. Several compartments were doused with petrol. A funeral pyre blazed through the train. Charred bodies were caged in twisted, hot metal frames.

"My father, Nikhil Jain, was among the fifty-seven dead," Jain said.

News of the train massacre reached Ahmedabad. The following day, on the twenty-eighth of February, avenging Hindus went on a rampage—burning, looting and savagely killing anyone suspected to be a Muslim. If there was doubt about a male suspect, he was forced to reveal his penis. The circumcised were hacked to death.

"I was in my home with mother Maya when I learnt of the tragedy."

We held our breath as we listened to Jain.

"My second mother died six months later ... in her sleep. I think from grief."

Jain finished his electric narrative.

Yuri hung his head in silence. He made the sign of the cross. Farooq sat silent as a stone, his fist clenched beneath his chin. Milli's gaze remained on Jain.

Mr. Jain lowered his voice. "I made a promise then that both my fathers, Rahim and Nikhil, will live on."

He continued. "The voice is mine, but not the words. I feel it. Someone else moves my tongue and guides my feet ..."

As if I too had lost my voice to someone else, I uttered these words: "Greatness is its own guide."

Jain rose. He came over to me and held me in a quiet embrace. I felt his warm glow. I felt Milli's eyes on me.

Snakes and Ladders

The light is in every heart and the tool to travel the experience of the universe. [Bhagavad-Gita]

Our particular aspirations varied. Farooq chose civil service to be an honest spokesman for his people. Milli became a journalist, and I a writer. Yuri, who was a one world, one nation person, had set his mind on cultural anthropology. Our pathways to various goals crossed each other's. We shared a few common lecture courses at JNU. We were halfway through Jain's course on world religion and philosophy, enigmatically named Snakes and Ladders. Yet we were dissimilar in so many ways. The common denominator that held us together remained elusive to me.

On a rather dull day, we sat at a small table in the college cafeteria. Milli complained about her mother being away so long. Our heads propped on books, we waited for a reviving cup of afternoon tea. Sweltering heat added to our torpor. I was divvying up the relative guilt of the thermal and the didactic when Yuri asked what I had meant to ask all along.

"What keeps us together? Do we all sense a common purpose?"

"Why does it have to be so complicated? We have chemistry," Milli said. She wanted to keep things simple.

"Born a Hindu, I tend to be fatalistic. I keep thinking our meeting Jain the first two times was not an accident." I looked at Milli as I brought forth the notion.

"What happens by chance does not have to be preordained," said Milli.

"Look, he is a charmer, he has a big brain sitting over a handsome face, he is a magnet. We can't deny that," Farooq interjected.

"Well, let us see what we have learned from his lectures," I said as I attempted to change the topic.

I summarized. "From Jain's Snakes and Ladders, we learn that, as in the children's board game, the purpose in life is to get to square one hundred. Your actions and beliefs either got you up the ladder toward the perfect score or you fell into a snake's belly and had to start over. Jain firmly believes religion is philosophy. Ignore evangelical pulpit thumping. Religion is a catalyst for contemplation, not a fattah for faith, he says."

"God feels asphyxiated by our emotional tight squeeze on religion." It was Farooq who carried on. "Blind adherence to dogma placed the mind in a prison and stirred nations to irrational war and strife."

"Have you read The Passages, the pamphlet he distributed on the first day of his class? Nice quotes," Milli said.

Though our curiosity about Jain had only increased with each encounter, we still had our misgivings.

"Too good to be true," Farooq said, expressing his doubts.

"Interesting stuff." Yuri was undecided.

When I said, "I am a believer," Milli surprised me.

She said, "You fall for everything, Gora."

Suddenly, Milli jumped from her chair. She had spotted a dying insect near the door. Someone may have inadvertently trampled on one wing of the six-legged creature. It was making a dying effort to turn upright and fly away. "It is so sad to see them suffer." Milli walked resolutely to the door. She grimaced as she crushed the dying insect with her foot.

Our plastic tea cups in hand, we headed to another class with Jain. Milli stopped frequently on the way. At each stop, she rubbed the sole of her offending shoe against the sparse turf. "Go on, I will catch up," she told us.

Usually Milli, Yuri, Farooq, and I sat near each other somewhere in the midsection of Jain's classroom. Never upfront. If one of us was absent for a session, Jain noticed and would ask, "Where is so and so today?"

Bulbul, fidgety as the bird she was named after, always sat in the front row. She had black wavy hair reaching below her shoulders and a rather plain face that was pretty when she smiled, though she smiled rarely. She raised her hand each time Professor Jain said anything sounding heretical. We joked about her back-and-forth with the professor and named it The Bulbul-Jain Dialogue.

When Jain said, "Islam is viewed by many today as the most intolerant of the widely practiced religions," Bulbul interrupted.

"Sir, are you partial to any one religion?" she asked.

"It is reasonable to assume that God is not partial to one human being over another or to one creed over another. We too should remain impartial," Jain said.

Bulbul raised her hand.

"You berate religion," she said. "Should we all become

The Last Day of Ramadan

atheists?"

"Thoughtful convictions more than religious affiliation keep us steady on the true path. The intellectually dead have no doubts—they fall in the adder's mouth. Only the curious can climb all the ladders," Jain answered.

"You must always be prepared. The unprepared run helter-skelter," Jain had said once when he was speaking about Jesus.

"What about miracles? Don't miracles prove that religion is more than philosophy?" Bulbul had asked.

"In my lifetime I have not heard of or seen one," said Jain. He paused. "The world needs a miracle more than ever now, wouldn't you agree?"

In one of his classes, I framed a basic question with this poem:

Like a bastard, fatherless—
helpless
like an orphan—
my mother, my father—
will you tell me?

Who breathes life
into this atom
this quark
this magic
of chance
of change
electric
pulsing like a quasar

dying like a falling star?
Will I know? Or will you tell me?

"No one knows the answer to that question, Gora. Perhaps when the cycle of evolution is complete, we will know the answer," Jain replied.

When the discussion on soul came up, Jain said, "Think of the Cartesian quote 'Cogito ergo sum; I think, therefore I am.' But what of the man who has suffered a devastating stroke, a hemorrhage into the cognitive cortex? Tied securely in the wheelchair—limbs flaccid, tongue drooping, saliva dripping on to his chest—has he ceased to exist before his death? He does not think, therefore he is not?" Jain was making us think.

I noticed Milli shake her head in affirmation.

"The real question is not whether we exist," Jain went on, "but whether we still exist after we are dead. After the EEG is a straight line but the heart beats, do we still exist? After death, when we cease to think, does the soul still exist, and where? At what point in the death process does the soul leave the body. Before rigor mortis? After rigor mortis or after cremation or burial? What is the soul? Can it exist without a body?"

This was deep stuff.

"In human individuality, the whole is greater than the sum of its chemical parts. Is the difference between the whole and the sum of parts the soul? A family that loses its abode—be it a humble tent among the refugees of Sudan or a mansion on a hilltop in Malabar Hills looking down on the people of the valley—is without a home. A home ceases to exist without the abode. Can the soul exist without its house, the body? Human cloning could be a revealing theological experiment. Will the clone have a soul? Who imparts the clone its soul? Is it shared?"

With these questions leaving us thinking, Jain ended the lecture.

1.618...The Divine Ratio

That which is not comprehended by the mind but by which the mind comprehends—
know that to be Brahman. [Upanishad]

A month later, after another religion and philosophy class, I was alone on the steps of the library when Jain came by and sat next to me. I asked him then if he pictured God in any particular form of matter or energy when he sat down to pray. I myself have imagined God as a very large man with flowing robes, a large beard, and a bald head. At times God is a single eye against a red sky. At times God is a misty cloud with undefined, ever-expanding edges, radiance behind the mist giving the impression of immense power. Occasionally, in my attempt to visualize God, I see the smiling face of my father. During moments of meditation, I have perceived God as an ever-expanding transparent ball of energy. I expected Jain to laugh aloud after my narration. He listened with interest.

I asked him, "What lies beyond space? Where does space end?"

"Space ends where future begins," Jain said.

These profound out-of-the-box answers increased my admiration of Jain more than I was willing to admit during that first year of our acquaintance.

The Last Day of Ramadan

Dusk approached as we sat there on the steps of the library. Jain said, "I think of God as a trillion arms rotating like a wheel and always moving forward. After all four of my parents died, I was alone, confused, and angry. I never forgot my father Jain's words: 'When you grow up, you will know love and hate and you will choose the better of the two.' Over time the meaning of my father's words sank in."

I don't recall if it was on that occasion or another that Jain had said, "When the personal god becomes the personal idol, feared more than loved, confusion sets in. Reason is a sharp weapon, Gora. It separates the true from the false."

I do remember that it was while we sat on the library steps that Jain gave me the first hint that he was on a mission and that he wanted the four of us to be part of it. He did not elaborate, but I recall him saying, "Be prepared, Gora. There will be events that will require that you are prepared. Yuri, Farooq, and Milli too will take part in this."

Jain was deep in thought. For several minutes he remained silent. I wondered what drove Jain to action: reason or love. I wondered then if greatness was Jain's mark. I looked at his eyes—the depth, the brightness, the intensity. What did Peter see when he looked at Jesus?

Jain said then, "You are a poet, Gora. To a poet, feeling is more pervasive, a more powerful argument than reason. Truly love seeks reason and reason discovers through love. I respect Rousseau. He lived the emotion of reason."

Thus far I was totally in line with Jain's train of thought. What threw me off the track was what he said next.

"As art and science blend to create a masterpiece, both love and reason are essential to great philosophy. We cannot see God, we cannot prove his existence by reason, yet we can feel him. The feeling is individual and collective. It is a genetic call to the prime source."

The pitch of his voice betrayed his anguish.

"The fight over God is crippling mankind. Religion is infiltrating media and big business. There is money in religion. The next onslaught will test our mettle. We must become one and equal before that imminent encounter. We will come face to face with the true aliens. We prepare or we perish."

I was shaken. Up to this moment, I had not judged the words that fell from Jain's mouth unkindly. This was different. Genetics! Onslaught! Aliens?

A nudge of doubt shook the absolute respect I held for Jain's intellect. I had heard Yuri ridicule philosophers. "They trap themselves in point and counterpoint, then try to extricate themselves from the prison of their own abstract design."

Our genetic link to God! Truly that was original. Yet, I was not ready to surrender fully. I was searching for the thorn in the rose bush. What did Jain mean by aliens? Aliens from outer space? Or those we have alienated? I juggled with doubting Jain and with self-doubt.

I shared the details of this encounter with Yuri, Farooq, and Milli during the lunch hour the next day.

I could see Milli was a convert.

"This is a man of destiny," she declared as I finished my exposé.

"Teaching is his writing on the tablet. Just wait and see. He will take us to the mountaintop," she prophesied.

"An iconoclast," Farooq said.

"Society kills the iconoclast before putting him on the cross," said Yuri.

I remembered when I was in the seventh grade in middle school, a particular teacher of social studies, whose name I will not divulge—I sort of liked him—tended to rattle off advice as though he had received the commandments on a very high mountain where the bush burnt and divine proclamation—in Hindi—came from an unseen voice—deep and foreboding: "Do this, do that, not that ..." and so on occupied the entire forty minutes of one of his classroom sessions. That night, as I slept with my notebook of "Do this, do that" beside my pillow, a chorus of cockroaches crept out of a crevice between the door and the cemented white wall. One after another a cockroach crawled out, tested the air with its dark antennae, and began to fly around my bed in brief oval circles.

The noise of the flying roaches woke me. I sat upright in bed, soaked in horror, not knowing what to do. I clutched the notebook in my hand. Panicked as I was, I began to flail at the flying roaches with the notebook. It was all I could do. What a relief! The roaches reentered the crevice one by one. The chorus ended. Relief at last!

My recall of the roach event at that precise moment—I am not fond of roaches in or out of their podium—baffled me. Was it Milli's eulogy? Was it Farooq's tribute or Yuri's Delphic prophecy?

Perplexed though I was, I respected Jain. I could not deny that in his class I felt the way I did when reading Dante's Inferno. I was in the company of greatness. But then there was

Milli. And I was young. To spill my brain and admit that in Jain I had found the master was unthinkable. I would rather submit to a spinal tap.

Jain would take us up to the mountaintop? Ridiculous! I would resort to practical psychology. This was the moment! It was time to test my idea. A change of scene would allay the confusion that muddled our minds. The professor would be put to the test. I would invite Jain to the high mountains! The Himalayas!

Later in the evening, I talked to Yuri and Farooq. "Let's go to the mountains. The semester ends in six weeks. My uncle has a small cottage in Kalimpong. We can spend a week there. Let's invite Jain to come with us. The Himalayas will reveal his true nature."

Yuri raised his eyebrows. I explained. "Kalimpong is sixty miles east of Darjeeling. It is a cute little hill station. After unpacking at my uncle's cottage, we will ride a Jeep to the foot of Tiger Hill. A little past four in the morning, our half-hour trek up the steep mountain will take us to the top of a flat lookout hill. There! Behold the presence of God as the blue light breaks into sunrise red. The golden thigh! Kanchenjungha!"

"You, a sun worshipper, Gora?" Yuri jabbed.

"Only the poet perceives God, Yuri. Not the theologian, not the mathematician, not the philosopher. A poet makes sense of reality. He gives abstract numbers meaning. Faith is but hope taking a blind leap. Math cannot go past the speed of light. The philosopher holds a string to the sky without a kite at its end. Only the poet's dream takes quantum leaps beyond matter and energy."

The Last Day of Ramadan

Yuri, who is built like a leopard on two legs, wrestled me to the ground. He was being playful. Nothing else would have silenced my pontification. None have seen the golden thigh of the Himalayas and not become a poet and a believer.

"You won't hear a word of poetry on the trip," I promised, trying to break his hold.

"That will be too bad," said Yuri as he let go.

The next day I called after Jain as he headed toward the faculty building. "Come with us to Kalimpong and Tiger Hill. You will see the divine when you behold the Kanchenjungha."

He turned his head and without hesitation said, "I will come."

Smugly satisfied, I left for my dorm room. The change of scene and the cool breeze would free the imprisoned philosopher. The divine ratio embedded in the golden peak would transform Jain.

Before Tiger Hill

To those who are good to me, I am good; to those who are not good to me, I am also good—thus all get to be good. [Lao-tze]

Plane tickets to Bagdogra were booked for the day after semester's end, a month and a half after my offer to take our group to my uncle's cottage in Kalimpong. Details of the trip were planned. A reserved Jeep would take us from Bagdogra/Siliguri to the hill station in the Himalayas. Milli had her suitcase and knapsack packed and ready for every possible surprise that could confront us. For an unmarried Indian girl of Milli's age to accompany four unmarried men on a field trip that lasted beyond the next sunrise, it would start a ripple of gossip. Society had to be placated. Milli cajoled Khoka, her cousin, to accompany us on this trip. He was twelve. He would endure our mature company. A trek to the mountains was sufficient compensation. But events set back the clock. A week before our flight to Bagdogra, we rushed to Safdarjang Hospital on Milli's call. Her father had suffered a stroke. The trip to Tiger Hill did not take place for another year.

There he was, Milli's father, helpless in a hospital bed. A plastic tube inserted in his throat connected him to the ventilator. Intravenous lines ran from his arms up to yellow and milky fluids held in plastic bags. His right arm lay limp at his side. The right leg was motionless. Tears ran from his half-open right eye.

As I watched him, a thought crossed my mind: this is how a father feels when he has outlived his son. If a bus accident killed me today, my father would succumb and lie helpless in the same manner, dangled between this world and the next. This was more than a stroke—a scalpel had cut through the surgeon's brain and severed his soul from his mind. I think? I am?

Other thoughts engaged my mind. Is the soul dead when the brain is cut in half? My pet cockatiel injured herself flying into a glass window. A part of her feathery scalp became bald. When, at the end of my school day, she heard the school bus come to a halt in front of our house, the cockatiel would limp to the front door to greet me. She sensed my presence when the school bus came. She wanted to be stroked on the baldness where the injury had left her featherless. She wanted love. Leave soul out and Descartes seemed to make sense. There was no soul—dead or alive—only sense and sensibility. Doubt had invaded my brain.

Milli watched over her father day and night. Her father had saved many lives at this hospital. Nurses and technicians were devoted to giving the doctor the best shot at recovery. They turned him, sponged him, and fed him liquids with a straw. We took turns. Yuri, Farooq, and I relieved Milli from her grim watch-post so she could grab a bite to eat and take a shower. We brought magazines to occupy her time. They piled up on a chair in the corner of the hospital room.

Jain visited Milli's father at the hospital one evening. He put his hand on the suffering surgeon's forehead. I could see the look on Milli's face. She was expecting a miracle. Stupid girl!

I relented. I could be forgiving. She was going through such turmoil.

Jain spoke softly. "You will get better, Papa. You have healed so many."

The helpless surgeon smiled wryly. He tried to raise his right hand to grip Jain's. The tip of his fingers quivered. He gave up and looked away.

It was a week before Milli's mother could catch the plane from Baltimore to New Delhi. I had gone to the Indira Gandhi International Airport to pick her up. I was prepared to carry a large piece or two of luggage. Instead, when she exited customs, she held in her hand one small suitcase.

"How long will you stay, Aunty?" I asked instinctively.

She said, "I don't know, Gora." I watched her face as she said this. I knew. She knew too.

A few years back, I had read a poem written by a friend several years older than me. He was training to be a neurologist. A patient under his care as an intern had suffered a stroke, a "CVA," short for cerebrovascular accident, he had called the condition. As the patient lay helpless in bed, not unlike Milli's father, his wife who had been away and who had rushed back to town held his hand with one of her hands and wiped tears with the other. All the while she kept mumbling words of comfort to her husband, knowing well that he could not hear or comprehend what she said. He was on the respirator and his condition was deteriorating. For a brief moment, before the monitor declared him dead, the patient miraculously opened his eyes and looked at his wife.

"Believe me, Gora," my neurologist friend said, "it was

a miracle—or telepathy only mentalists are capable of. I have never seen anything quite like it ever again."

On that evening of the patient's death, my friend wrote a poem which he shared with me later. After reading it, I suggested to him that he name the poem "The Ventriloquist." I had a copy of it. I read it to Yuri and Farooq. I did not think Milli would handle it well then.

The half-empty bag
hung from polished chrome pole
pumped fluid hope
into his arm—pale and limp.
As she walked in and held his hand,
the huff-puff bellow beside the bed,
arrested halfway—sighed again—
—again.
He looked beyond me,
hunched over him with my stethoscope,
to where she sat holding his hand—
reproached her long absence
then mellowed soft as love.
This I swear,
this I heard
distinct as death:
"I did wait.
It hasn't been long—
the petal's fresh, the scent strong,
for you I have held these roses."

The sparse baggage collected, Pamela and I went directly to the hospital. When Milli's mother entered the room, holding on to Milli as though the two needed all four legs to stand, the doctor lay speechless on his hospital bed, his right hand twitching occasionally. He repeatedly pulled on the bed sheet with his left hand, attempting to cover himself—his feeble attempt to reestablish his dignity.

Milli's father looked at them. He shook his head. He tried to speak. Tears welled from his eyes. He did not take his eyes off them.

"I am here to take care of you. I will never again leave you alone. You worked too hard. I was always afraid," Pamela said as she held her husband's hand.

Pamela opened her suitcase and looked into it as a carpenter into a toolbox. With great deliberation, she took out a nurse's apron, tied the straps around her waist, and went to work.

I had guessed. The small suitcase was not the hint of a brief stay—it spoke of how little she needed to sustain herself. The fear that had kept her away now bound her to the same life that she once ran away from.

Walk Like a King, Talk Like a Poet

Behold, there went out a sower to sow ... as he sowed, some seeds fell by the way side ... And some fell on stony ground, where it had not much earth; and immediately it sprang up ... But when the sun was up, it was scorched; and because it had no root, it withered away ... [Gospel of Mark: Parable of the Sower]

While we waited for our trip to the Himalayas, we spent many Saturday evenings at Rajah's, as we had done before we met Jain. On occasions we would invite the professor to join us, and he did so eagerly. Jain had not called on us explicitly to be his faithful followers. He had not said, "Come follow me if you wish to inherit the kingdom to come." He had however dropped a hint here and there, and, between the lectures and our private conversations, we perceived that a mission was unfolding and that he wanted us to be a part of it.

To Yuri he had said, "Sermons will not solve intolerance and the deaths it causes. I have met a Delhi tycoon, a self-made man, who has many personal problems that he is unable to solve even with his riches. He too is bigoted. He could have been our instrument for social change."

Farooq had shared this with us. Jain had told him, "Muslims killing Muslims! We have to stop people killing each other in the name of God. When the time comes and I am ready, I will ask you to join me."

When classes resumed, Jain preached more forcefully for change. The world was unprepared for the inevitable escalation of unrelenting savagery—that was his message. He did not chalk out a visible plan of action, but it was clear to the four of us that he had chosen us to carry out his act of retribution or redemption.

"Something has to be done" was Jain's mantra. What? Jain was elusive as to the particulars. What was expected of us? He did not know.

Farooq said, "Gora, maybe we are putting ourselves in the imagined position of activists."

I replied, "Our indoctrination has begun. We will be Jain's disciples."

A minute later I said, "I don't know what made me say that, Farooq."

Among us, Milli was resolute in her faith in Jain. She never disparaged the professor.

A month before we departed for Kalimpong, we sat in a circle on the grass lawn in front of the Library—Milli, Yuri, Farooq, and I. We had decided that we would put our doubts to rest. The afternoon class had ended. Soon Jain came out of the faculty room and sat down beside us. We approached him point-blank as planned.

"How is one to prepare for an action one has no inkling as to what it is?" I asked.

"Walk like a king, talk like a poet," Yuri preempted Jain.

"Think like a philosopher," Milli appended as she chewed on a blade of grass.

Jain smiled. "If you see a child with palsy drooling saliva along his chin, you are either repulsed or you wipe his face gently with a kerchief. If someone throws a stone at you, you pick another and hurl it at his head or you walk away without fear in your footsteps. This is preparation: being ready to do what you would want to do."

Hearing this, Farooq stood up and beat his chest and back with his fists. He said with mock fortitude, "I am ready. Tell me what I have to do."

"The sage is in the savage," Jain said as he held his fist against his heart. "Prepare not just to tame the savage but to train it."

"That is our mission. If we are prepared, we will know how to act when the moment comes. From the very first days when I met you at the café, I have known you to be true to yourselves. I have embraced you with open arms. The moment will come. When it is ripe, I will call you."

Jain had never been clearer than this about his mission and our role in it, hazy as the details remained. Months from now, when Yuri and I would have our first encounter with Mr. Syed Musa on the quadrangle of Jama Masjid, the outlines of our mission would become distinct, and foreboding.

Farooq said, "A third war is no longer unthinkable. Bush's crusade has bit the dust. If Iran underestimates America's resolve, Tehran will fare no better than Baghdad. What can a few do? Can the four of us hold the ocean at bay with a page of your book, sir?"

We were prepared for point-blank questions—this was loaded artillery. Leave it to the irrepressible Farooq Shahjehan.

Jain answered, "He will win who makes the aggressor see the innate error of his planned attack—the corruption in the core of his belief. He will win who remains true to his own beliefs and refuses to allow the enemy to corrupt him, Farooq."

"You will be the guardian of my message," Jain ended.

Transfiguration

Everything changes, everything appears and disappears.
Transcend both life and extinction, ascend the tranquil peak. [Buddha]

On a hazy Sunday morning, a year to the day since the former set date, we headed to the airport—Milli, her cousin Khoka, Farooq, Yuri, Jain, and I. As we waited for our flight at the airport lobby, Milli pulled me aside.

"Something is about to happen, Gora. I feel it."

"Don't worry," I assured her.

"Your mother will look after your dad. We will be gone a mere seven days. Delhi will be the same seven days from now."

"I don't mean my father. I mean something big is going to happen on this trip," she whispered.

I squeezed her hand reassuringly. Feminine fancy. She was under so much strain.

A year had passed since Milli's father had suffered his stroke. In doctor lingo, his condition was stable. His intelligence had diminished to childlike simplicity; his conversation was repetitive. When we went to visit him, he would ask what our names were. A second after you answered he would ask again. At times he did not recognize Milli.

"I have a daughter," he would tell her.

He would ask Milli, "Where is your father? What does he do?"

When asked how he was, unable to get the words out, he would hang down his head. He would squeeze his forehead with his left hand, trying to force out the thoughts that instinct prompted should be there. Strangely, he never failed to recognize his wife—never asked her who she was. Whenever he was in distress, or in need of food or water, he called for "Pammy." If Pamela was out of sight for more than a few minutes, he would bang a spoon against the tabletop, anxiety adding to melancholy on his palsied face. Pamela would come in and say, "Now, now." There was no rebuke in her voice.

We decided it was time to go on our trip. It would be good for Milli.

An hour after take-off, our plane landed at Bagdogra. Our knapsacks and duffels were loaded onto a Tata Safari. By noon, we were on the road to Kalimpong.

BRO signs marked the turns: "Be Gentle on my Curves." "If you are married don't hurry, your wife can wait." BRO, our driver pointed out, stood for Border Road Corporation, a government agency. Our married man at the wheel ignored all cautionary road signs. Winding around small hills and jig-jagging up the side of broad mountains, the Jeep reached new heights and opened vistas of grandeur at each turn. The Jeep ride edged past three hours.

A child looks up to his or her father. Men and women look up to the mountain—the mountain was Dad and the Himalayas the grandest dad of all. On the narrow curving roads, our heads tossed to one side on a turn and to the other on the next. As the Jeep struggled uphill on its steep climb, the mind was stirred to a higher level of consciousness. Flat roads trudge through reality; on uphill climbs the experience was of the sublime.

Yuri wondered if the Urals were just as pretty. He had never been there.

Here and there a spring cut its clear path down the jagged face of rocks and caught the sun. Farooq craned his head till the last reflection disappeared into the bend of the road. Jain, who usually had his head buried in a book, looked to the mountains with the intensity of a vision. When the sun cut through a gap in the hills, the serenity of his face caught the halo.

Milli whispered into my ears. "Remember how he spoke of Jesus and the Transfiguration in class? It reminds me of that."

Hungry Mountains

After Jesus had roamed the wilderness without food or water for forty days and forty nights, the Devil came to him and said, "If you are the Son of God, turn these stones to bread." Jesus replied, "Man cannot live by bread alone." [Gospel of Matthew]

I would not condone idol worship. Milli's transgression from a forward-thinking modern woman to one with seducible immaturity infuriated me. True, she was under stress. A sinking feeling in the pit of my stomach robbed the mountains of their grand eloquence. A small bump on the road can unsteady a man's tread and throw him off the sublime precipice. Frankly, I was puzzled.

In another tortuous hour we reached the cottage. Yuri and Farooq jumped out of the Jeep.

"At last," said Farooq as he stretched his arms and legs.

"I will love this place. A nice little cottage on the lap of a mountain," said Yuri.

As the driver unloaded the Jeep, Jain chatted with the caretaker of the cottage. My eyes stayed with Milli. I thought of her small breasts against me on the steps of JNU. I would warn her of the dangers of hero-worship at the first appropriate opportunity. Being too critical could turn her against me. To that point, we dated but we had not spoken of love or gone beyond holding hands.

A big black beetle lay belly up on the verandah in front of the main door to the cottage. It was either dead or dying; I could not tell from where I stood. Milli had seen the insect. She walked to the verandah and bent over it. From her expression, I sensed that the insect was still alive. Milli lifted the insect by the tip of its wing and gently placed it in one far corner of the balcony, out of harm's way. The annoyance her whispered words had provoked in me eased a bit.

I did not fail to notice Milli's opposite responses in dealing with a dying insect. I thought, I am making a mountain out of an insect because everything Milli does is important to me. In the first instance she was missing her mother and was vexed.

After saving the dying insect, Milli and Khoka walked to the back of the cottage. I was tired after the journey. There was much on my mind. The caretaker had placed two aluminum-framed recliners on the lawn in front of the cottage. I went over and sat down on one of them. The grandeur of the mountain was hypnotic. Soon I fell asleep.

You can go to bed with fantasy; you cannot make love to it. Stars are fantasies; the moon is reality. Everyone is in love with the moon. Men and women, or as Yuri would say mwen, are equally enraptured by the moon. Whether you see the moon ride over a meadow, sail over the sea, or wobble between voids in the cityscape, the moon is your lover. The moon was bouncing between mountains tonight, and I wanted to make love to her.

The Jeep driver's shouts broke my trance. I cannot say how much time had passed. It must have been a while because the sky had darkened and I found myself alone. The baggage had been moved inside. A few stars were faintly visible. He was yelling at Farooq.

"You could get killed!" he was admonishing. "What if I did not happen to pass that road at that precise time? You would be dead. Hill people can be ferocious—tough as the mountains. They are proud people and don't hesitate to use their bhojali [curved dagger]. If I was not there, your gut would be trailing the ground. Vacation would be over."

I jumped out of the recliner to learn what had fanned the driver's fury.

Three whorls down the mountain road, five hundred or so feet below our cottage, the hill people lived in a nest of small cottages. Farooq went for a stroll down the mountain road before the sun set. Women who worked the tea gardens returned home about then. Two women, secure in the belief that the shrubs and trees surrounding their cottage provided adequate privacy, were bathing in the nude at the back of their home. Farooq had moved in to get a closer look at this Gauguinesque simplicity. He was there but a moment, his head protruding between two tree trunks, when the older of the two women spotted him.

Farooq told me later, "She smiled at me, Gora. I smiled back. What else was I supposed to do?"

The woman pointed him out to the younger one who, while grabbing at the closest piece of garment, shrieked in panic at the sight of Farooq relishing her nakedness.

"The younger girl started to scream. Two men rushed out of the cottage. I started to run," Farooq had confided later.

"Lucky I was passing by," the driver said. "I saw your friend run past me. Two men were chasing him, one with a bhojali. I was scared but I stopped them. I told them I knew him and he was good boy. I slipped a few ten-rupee notes into the hands of the angry men. That settled the matter."

With gratitude I gripped his hands.

The driver had vouched for Farooq. He was a good boy. The moon can play havoc on a young mind. Farooq was faultless in my eyes—just curious.

Soon the stars were brighter. I looked for Milli. I spotted her at a distance coming back toward the cottage. She was with Jain, Khoka, and Yuri.

Seeing me, she shouted, "We went for a walk! Khoka could hardly wait a second. Everything is lovely. We did not wake you."

Our Jeep driver repeated a bravado description of the happenings as soon as the four reached the front door. Yuri beat his chest chimpanzee fashion. He promised to get Farooq hitched to a mountain bride before the trip ended. Farooq was so embarrassed by the incident that he made no protest. He went inside the cottage. I did not follow. Let him be alone. Sort his nerves!

Soon the darkness spread a grimace on the mountain face. We were to leave for Tiger Hill at three a.m. As we stuffed and zipped our knapsacks, the caretaker warned us to check our shoes before putting them on in the morning. On occasion, a snake found comfort in the warmth and snugness of a shoe if the night got chilly. In the Himalayan hills, snakes are not a rarity.

After a light supper of curried chicken and rice, we went to sleep early. I wondered if Farooq lay awake, unable to fall asleep.

Would he have nightmares or pleasant dreams? He seemed deep in sleep. He was a good boy. Just curious.

I lay awake for a while. I tossed and turned, my mind beset with small things.

That night, lying in the lap of the cold mountain where the fir trees cast long and distorted shadows, I had a nightmare. I wrote a poem about it after we had returned to New Delhi.

The avalanche of events that followed the first night in Kalimpong may have influenced the macabre attributes of my dream.

> *Suspended in a room—*
> *test-tube shaped, larger*
> *and without visible exits,*
> *my feet dangle—*
> *strings*
> *on a birthday balloon.*
>
> *With each beating of my breath*
> *the glass walls expand and fall*
> *in rhyme with birds outside*
> *flapping their wings,*
> *flying upwards, away*
> *and back again*
> *to rest their claws*
> *on cracked crevices in the glass.*
>
> *As night folds over me,*
> *a mosquito net of sorts—*

The Last Day of Ramadan

the birds claw the glass
desperate to tear in—
into my flesh
still suspended in the jar.

Along a cord hung from the top
a melody descends,
both sweet and mournful,
and falls to the floor—
a child's rhyme etched on my brain,
lingered refrain that will sustain
when the ghost-beast
claws the wall again.

Without apparent event or action on my part,
the creatures vanish, the walls bellow out—
a breath of relief.
I take in deep
—a sigh.
Instantly, the floor touches my feet.

The alarm went off at three. I was awake when it rang, unable to sleep well after the bad dream. Our chosen outfits were beside our beds. We were ready in a hurry. The Jeep was on its way not long after. I watched the eerie lights of the Jeep peer and peek around the bends on the mountain road.

An hour later, the Jeep clanked to a stop in a graveled parking space.

It was past four when, knapsacks on our back, we started

our climb along the pebbled path. The night was clear and cloudless. The quarter moon was spread lightly on the well-trod path. We used our flashlights sparingly, relishing the faint menace of uncertainty.

The path was strewn with stones and rocks. At a bend, I stumbled on a rounded pebble and fell toward the path's edge. Milli was close behind me. She lunged forward and grabbed me by the knapsack. We both fell, she on top of me.

"Gora, be careful. You have a great story to write."

"What story?" I asked her.

"The story of the hungry mountain," she said as she got up, pulled down her blouse, and resumed her climb. I brushed off the dirt and ran to catch up with the others—our group and forty or so other men and women who had gathered on the flat top of Tiger Hill to watch the sunrise. We waited for the moment. From time to time, someone took his hands out of deep overcoat pockets to pull a scarf more warmly around his or her neck. A woman sneezed once. It sent a chill through my spine. It was cold.

Sunrise is hope waking after a night of darkness—nowhere with more color than over the Kanchenjungha. Once seen, the image is digitalized—eleven megapixels imprinted on the somnolent retina—to be replayed over and over and over. The sketch of a grandmaster etched with a peacock feather—the only thing that can surpass this experience is coming face to face with God.

Everyone had a camera out. Jain too was storing this image in his pocket Olympus. It was tiny. It did not possess the wide-angled scope to extend the vistas of colors, shapes, and shadows over the expansive dimension—the grandeur iridescent in every detail of light. Jain stepped back. He looked through the lens again. He stepped back five steps. Then four more. A woman shrieked. The sunrise escaped the camera and Jain disappeared below the horizon.

I ran down the slope to where he lay. Yuri and Farooq followed close behind me.

Milli shouted after us, "Gora, be careful!"

The trunk of a cedar had deflected his fall. Jain lay against a rock some thirty feet below the flat lookout point of Tiger Hill. Motionless. Nothing moved except the trickle of blood from the gash on his forehead.

Enlightenment

He whose mind seeks the truth crosses the river of death and dying,
he unravels the secret of maya—he is dear to Me—he is one in Me. [Bhagavad-Gita]

The location is remote. Aside from the sizable military camps in the area, few households exist in the vicinity of Tiger Hill. We lifted the unconscious and oddly curled Jain from the ground where he lay to a makeshift stretcher made with light logs, and a length of rope our driver carried in his Jeep. He had sustained large bruises on his chest. His breath was easy and his pulse strong. About thirty feet up, we placed the makeshift stretcher on a clearing close to the observation area from where Jain had fallen. His right leg had rolled off the side of the stretcher. When I stretched his legs along the stretcher, he winced.

It was a while before the two-member ambulance crew arrived. They had rushed up the pebble path, leaving the ambulance in the parking area. Once the crew transferred Jain from the makeshift log stretcher to a secure one, the painstaking descent down the pebbled path to the parking area began. We descended slowly, planting each step firmly before taking the next. Jain lay unconscious on the stretcher. Occasionally he groaned. When he did, we felt relief. He was alive!

The Last Day of Ramadan

Yuri was at the lead. He took slow, deliberate steps down the hill, warning the others, "Be careful, we don't want to drop him." Farooq was unusually quiet. I think the passage of events from the past evening on had stunned him. So much had happened since our plane had landed at Bagdogra. Milli too was overwhelmed. She kept pulling on my shirt while asking me to slow down and to watch the rounded pebbles.

When we reached the parking space at the bottom of the hill, with Jain secure inside the ambulance, the driver started the engine. The ambulance crew advised it was best to take Jain to Darjeeling. The hospital there was equipped for reasonably modern services. I occupied a seat near the stretcher. I tightened my painful grip on the metal frame as frequent bumps on the uneven road sent shivers to my teeth. A bump in the road could worsen Jain's injury. Every thud and vibration made me remorseful and repentant—it was my plan that brought Jain to the mountains. It was my suggestion that had tempted Jain to Tiger Hill.

Yuri, Milli, Khoka, and Farooq followed in the Jeep.

Hours later Jain was admitted to the ICU in a Darjeeling hospital. A head CT scan showed a linear crack in the skull along the frontal bone. There was swelling of the brain. No internal bleeding was detected. No subdural hematoma was noted on the CT scan of the brain. Jain remained in coma.

The next day, Khoka returned to his parents in Delhi. Our mood was somber. After hours of watchful waiting at the hospital, we needed rest. None of us volunteered to go back to our cottage.

"Kalimpong is far by car. We won't be able to watch over

Jain." We agreed with Milli. We found rooms at the Everest Hotel.

Yuri suggested we take a walk around the mall to calm our nerves and make a suitable plan for Jain's care. To make the air light, he warned Farooq to stay a safe distance from Nepalese women.

Milli said, "Leave him alone, that poor boy."

Farooq was embarrassed, but he managed to spurt out, "I don't know what will leave the deeper impression on my soul: high mountains or the smaller ones."

Before I could open my mouth, he said, "Shut up, Gora."

We walked along Mall Road. The Kanchenjungha was visible from several lookout points along the road. Even our distressed minds felt the calm spread over the mountain's vastness. From time to time, wafts of cloud floated over the road and wrapped us in a blanket. We were together in this. I reached out and held Milli's hand. I felt her soul and mine as one. She left her hand in mine.

When the cloud passed and we had made the round of Mall Road, we were back at the hospital to decide how we would arrange Jain's immediate care.

Milli felt that he would get better medical care in Delhi. "My father did not recover from his stroke, but Jain may have a chance if we move him to Delhi."

We agreed. Jain had no relatives that we knew of. The doctor said it would be safe to transport him in a day or two as there was no evidence of any brain or internal hemorrhage. His limbs were bruised but not broken. Besides the hairline fracture on the frontal skull bone, only two ribs had cracks. No pneumothorax.

"Lungs are clear to percussion and auscultation. Stable hemoglobin and hematocrit," the young doctor wrote in the chart.

Three days later, Jain was moved to Bagdogra by ambulance. Later that day we were on the flight to New Delhi. When we reached Safdarjang Hospital, Jain was still comatose. The one reassuring sign of life was the steady sound of his breath.

Two weeks passed. We saw little progress. Whenever time permitted, we sat by Jain's bed in the hospital. I cannot explain it, but it was more than caring for a fellow man in an unpredictable state of health who had no one else to look after him. It was more than respect for a learned man. We were drawn to his room when we awoke in the morning. We thought of him when we went to bed at night.

Even Farooq, who was by nature lighthearted and outgoing, visited him each day. He held Jain's hand and spoke assuredly of his certain recovery. "You will rise again." He read the morning news to the comatose Jain, making sly remarks on topics that amused him.

We all talked to Jain though we knew he could not reply.

Yuri would say, as he wiped Jain's forehead with the bandana he was in the habit of wearing, "Listen to a Russian. Never give up. Not even Stalin could kill Russia."

Milli sat by the hospital bed in the evenings. Once I saw her weeping. Another time I saw her holding Jain's hand and looking into it as if she was reading a book. After a while, she leaned over and kissed Jain on the forehead.

The guilt and the uncertainty! I thought I was in hell till I remembered that Jain refuted the existence of hell.

"God is pure love. Pure love knows no anger. Without anger

and retribution there can be no hell. In God's presence, even the most hardened soul will feel remorse for his inaction or malice. Remorse is God's justice."

Jain was unaware of our presence. He did not speak. Rarely he moved his toes or fingers. He withdrew his limbs when provoked with a pin by the nurse as she came around to make her assessment. That was all. There was one hopeful sign: progress MRIs noted less brain swelling. One other: "Pupillary and tendon reflexes are brisk and intact," the doctor assured us. "No focal neurologic damage."

The neurologist was encouraged by these signs. "A skull fracture and a bad concussion," he said. "I have seen the dead rise, my friends. I have seen men weeks in coma rise and walk out of the hospital." He tried hard to put us at ease.

As days passed, our faith in the doctor's optimism waned. Each passing day convinced us that Jain would never recover. He would choke on the liquid the doctors fed him through a tube, catch pneumonia, become septic, and succumb to his preordained fate. Jain's mission would end before it began.

Jain told us later that it was during this "meditative state" that he had his vision.

The Last Day of Ramadan

Pose Like Dali

As fire is indispensable to cooking,
so is knowledge essential for deliverance. [Sankara-
charya]

My soul was dead. It was bereft of the slightest happiness. The sun rose and fell without casting light or shadow on my life. The trees, houses, and the sky were matted together—in one plane without depth. I brooded all day long. At the end, I had little recall of what thoughts had crossed my mind. I stayed in my dorm room, hunched over a book—over the same page for hours. I had no appetite for breakfast or lunch. I was not hungry.

We were fearful of Jain's poor prognosis, I as much as anyone else. The possibility that Jain would never recover his immense mental vitality darkened our days. Destiny propelled us forward when Jain was around. Before his accident, on the way to Kalimpong, he had said, "Being a professor of comparative religion has opened many doors to me. I have convinced several influential men and women that our cause is worthy and timely. I have yet to convince them of the need for urgent and decisive action."

On another occasion, when the Jeep had stopped on the wayside for Khoka to have a drink of cola, Jain said, "I have a plan brewing in my mind. It is sketchy. When I figure out the details of the plan, I will tell you."

Before Jain's fall off the cliff, though undecided on the precise roles we would play, the sense was real that the stage was being set. His coma had switched off the stage lights.

Those days, we visited Jain often at the hospital. It became a ritual. One evening, Milli and I planned to see a movie after visiting Jain. I had bought two tickets to the show. I was to meet her at the hospital. We would go to the cinema hall after our visit.

It was late in the afternoon when I reached Jain's room. Once again I found Milli holding his hands in the palm of hers. Innocent enough. She held her head so close to the palm of Jain's hand that I had the impression that she was about to entrust her entire life in the hand she was holding. She was so engrossed that it was several seconds before she realized I was there. Act one, scene one. After we left the hospital, I sat through the movie without saying a word. All through the movie, Milli kept her hand in mine. That act did not lift me from my insecurity.

I remained immersed in this languid mental state for weeks.

Yuri consoled me. "Milli will be yours to love and cherish, Gora."

What did he know?

"You will be a great writer," He said. "Hermann Hesse had long bouts of depression."

He had more trust in my abilities than I did at that moment. Yuri would make a great writer. Every Russian can be Tolstoy. Conflict is art.

For me though, my conflicts were the black poster of death hanging over my bedstead. No, not death! Much worse. Death and dying are acts of defiance or submission. I was in suspended animation—a dirty black shirt hung and forgotten on a clothesline across the balcony, left to collect more dust and grime.

I read little. I was falling behind in my class preparation. The sky was dark at night and the stars yellow blotches besmeared over the night face. The thought of Milli turned my gloom to despair worse than that of a mother holding a dead child. What little I wrote was noir.

Now I see you
as men and women
have seen in each
for thousand years—
your one face wrinkled
and the other taut,
your one cheek loose
and the other baby-bulged.
Now I say to you
what men and women
have said to each
for thousand years—
you and I will walk to the edge
where the earth falls into the lake
where life
reflects in a pool.

You and I have known this
and he before me
and she after—
this we were told before we were born.

What rubbish! I tore up the poem before anyone could read the stuff! Yuri came in as I was shredding the poem to its last hyphen.

"Come out of your cocoon, Gora. Pose with your soul bared before public view. Like the crazy artist, run wires through your hair and wrap your arms in a blood pressure cuff. Go to New York or Mumbai and pose from a studio window. You will be the Dali of writers." I was not consoled. Yuri left. He shrugged when near the door as if he was giving up on me.

The next morning Yuri came to my room again. "If you don't get up, put on a clean shirt and come out with me, I am going to strangle you."

I motioned that I did not care. Yuri came closer. He pulled me up by my shirt collar. I was half out of my chair. Yuri had the strength of a leopard. He put a choke hold around my neck. I could not breathe.

"Yuri, please let …" The words died before I could finish. He would not let go. His fingers tightened further.

"Please, Yuri." I tried to get away.

"See, Gora? You are not ready to give up." He let go of his chokehold.

Yuri's offensive was an instant cure for my mental torpor. It was the lift that I needed. From that moment on, I knew I would recover. The best way to make a child drink milk is to take it away from him.

O! The Fool!

The absurd is the essential concept of the first truth.
[Albert Camus]

This escapade took place three months after my recent encounter with Yuri. With husky intonation fit for a séance, Yuri mouthed this ditty.

Let there always be sunshine,
Let there always be sky,
Let there always be mama,
Let there always be me!

As he laid a deck of tarot cards on the square table before him, he explained that the song was popular in Stalin's Russia. I sat directly opposite the pretentious mystic—grim and portentous under a black bandana tied around his forehead. He was determined to revive my love of life and I was going to go along. I must say he resembled a pirate more than a soothsayer.

Yuri shuffled the deck of cards. With a magician's deliberation, he placed the top tarot card face up in the center of the table. "This is you," he said softly, distinctly. He shuffled the remainder of the deck once more and handed it to me. He asked me to shuffle the deck once. This done, I handed the deck back to Yuri. Preserving the gravity of the séance, I leaned to look at the card, face up on the table, without spilling my bubbling curiosity.

"My mother learnt tarot on a trip to Prague. She taught me." Yuri was intense. Many images were imprinted on the card.

"The Tower! It is you, Gora," Yuri mumbled.

Lightning had struck the summit and the base of the Tower was crumbling. A strange creature was pictured falling off the tower. A golden crown was crashing to the ground below.

"There will be chaos and confusion. It is so close. I feel it." Yuri was taking this very seriously.

My legs became numb as he spoke. The tottering Tower! I began to believe in tarot. Was I prepared for this experience? I was just beginning to recover from the dark days of melancholy …I drew six more cards from the pack, all of which Yuri placed face down on the table in a particular order. Yuri covered the Tower with one of the chosen six cards.

"This is your present." He placed the next card horizontally across the second. saying that was the "obstacle."

The third was placed north of the Tower. "The crown card is your potential destiny."

The fourth card, placed south of the Tower, was the feet—the tool of travel.

Yuri exposed each of the cards, seven in all, face up. He did so slowly and deliberately, making a commentary after each card was turned. A smudge of perspiration showed through the bandana on his forehead.

"This is behind you, your immediate past," Yuri explained as he placed the fifth card to the left of the tower. The last card he placed on the right. "Your future, Gora."

"Are you feeling okay?" I asked. "You are taking this too seriously."

"You are about to embark on a great journey," he continued as he turned the first card. He had ignored my inquiry.

"I see you embark on a great journey. It will take you be-

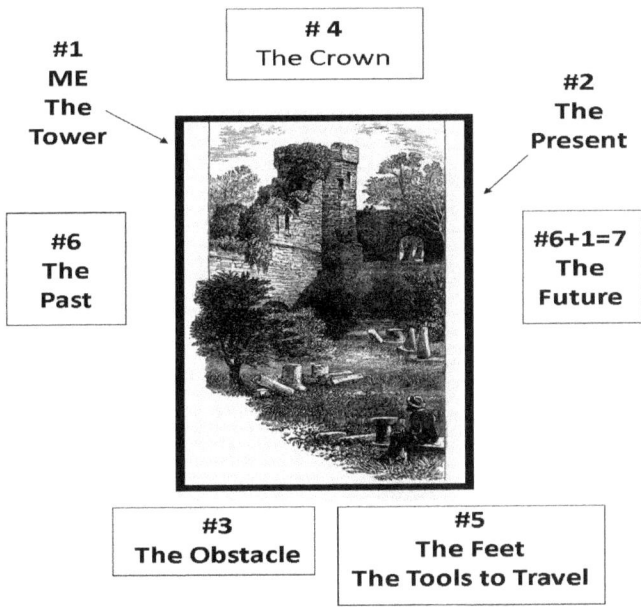

yond cities and mountains. I see a mountain rise. I see the peak turn into a steeple."

Yuri turned over the second card. The card was titled The Lovers. It pictured an angel looking over a man and a woman holding hands.

"You will be in a great partnership, Gora. I am in it too. I don't understand this. It makes me afraid." He paused.

He turned over the third card, which he had placed horizontally. Two sphinxes—one white, another black—flanked a rider on a chariot. Behind the chariot was a lush meadow, and beyond the meadow the star-laden cosmos hung over the outline of a city.

"The Chariot is your obstacle," he said. "But it came up inverted. Your hurdle may bring you speed."

"I don't understand all this," I mumbled.

"That's how tarot works," he said with seeming conviction as he placed his hand tentatively over the fourth card. "The meaning is hidden in the symbol."

The card in the crown position was The Moon afloat in the deep blue sky. The girl-face lying on the moon was not perturbed by the two jackals howling at her or by the two towers that strove to touch her. A crab clawed at the air above.

"I see spirits and unearthly things. I feel a chill in my spine." Yuri could be a practical joker. I smiled at his histrionics but resolved not to spoil his show.

Yuri seemed to relax when the "feet card" was turned over. The Sun was a smiling orb above the meadow. A cherub rode a white horse, a magic wand in his hand. Four sunflowers were bursting through the grass. Yuri said nothing. I felt a spirit hovering over me. It was spooky.

The card on the left—my past—was a blood-red heart against a granite sky. Three swords had pierced the heart. Large teardrops fell from the heart. Of the three swords, two were black, the third a shining steel. Chivalry? The black swords, who wielded them? Farooq? Jain? Could it be Yuri? He had said he was in it. Is that why sweat soaked his bandana? Perhaps it was not my heart. Was it Milli's? Was my shining steel sword failing to protect her? I waited for Yuri to explain.

"I know what you are thinking," Yuri spoke clearly. "You do not get the meaning of all this."

He had read my mind.

"You must trust your intuition. Your mind will not deceive if you …" His voice trailed off. With a sweaty palm he turned over the last card—the future. The World! Beads of sweat glistened on his flushed face.

"I feel the spirit," he said. "The spirit is breathing on my shoulders. Her breath is warm and cold. I am scared by it."

A garland encircled the card, and within the garland was a woman dancing. She was naked except for a silken scarf around her loin. The garland was indistinct. Was it made of roses or iron chain-links? I could not tell. Yuri was quite shaken. His hands were trembling visibly. I did not ask him what he read in the card.

"Terrible things will happen, Gora. Terrible …"

I did not let him finish. I knew what he was about to say.

"Pick one more card," I pleaded. "One more!"

"That's not how it is done."

"Just do it. For my sake. Please. One more!"

Yuri reached for the pack, his fingers tremulous. He pulled out a card from the middle of the pack and laid it face up on the table.

"For Jain," I shouted as he did so.

"O! The Fool!" I was amused. This thing was mighty foolish and The Fool turned up at the precisely right moment! As

I prepared to say so, I saw Yuri begin to tremble. His face was beet red with excitement. Beads of perspiration appeared on his neck. I desisted, perplexed. I looked at the card again. The red-robed fool, with a bag slung from a staff over his shoulder, stood at the edge of a precipice. He was about to take a long stride. His left hand held a white rose. His eyes showed no fear as they looked beyond the horizon.

"He is about to take a leap into the unknown." Saying this, Yuri slumped back in his chair. His body shook as if in a seizure. His eyes were open to the ceiling. I froze. I could not move till he stopped trembling.

"Where am I?" he asked.

"He is holding a white rose," I replied.

Yuri and His Woman

Love worketh no ill to his neighbor:
therefore love is the most fulfilling of law. [Romans 13:10]

I intimated earlier that Yuri was a good-looking man. He was naturally attractive to women. Many of the girls at JNU had their eyes on him. Yet he had not found the girl of his dreams. A fortnight after the séance, Yuri and I sat on a bench at Raj Ghat. We watched the orbic path of light dip behind the Jama Masjid. Yuri opened his heart.

"I need a beautiful woman in my life, Gora. Only women can make a man's life beautiful. God created woman. Man is the product of evolution."

I was prepared to concede that Yuri was defining women by their proclivity to tenderness and not by their sex organs. He set the matter straight.

"You are beautiful. Milli is beautiful. Farooq was beautiful before he fell on his ding-dong. He will redeem himself. He will meet his dream girl."

No, he was not talking about sex organs. But why did he mention the ding-dong? Was he thinking of Kalimpong?

"Jain is the most beautiful of all. Mark my word. I swear by the Dead Sea. Mark my word."

Sunset can play havoc on a mind.

"Before I came to India, I fell in love with a girl my age. She too was a student at the university. She was pretty. Oh, yes, she was pretty. She ran two miles a day, swam for an hour. She was angelic, like you say here, an apsara. I bought her inexpensive trinkets, and she was happy with that. She studied little but she was bright and caught on. Her father was a member of the Presidium. There lay our problem. I favored the inakomyshlyashchie, 'the other thinkers'—anarchists to the government.

"Everything was glorious for a while. It usually is. Then we began to argue about politics. We would be sitting on the grass watching the birds and admiring the flowers at the edges of the garden, when she would break the peace by a sudden proclamation that Russia should keep her romantic traditions. There was nothing wrong with having a czar! It was obsession. I was for a more modern Russia. She believed in status quo—'law and order,' she called it. I was in love. Ideology was in the way. She was beautiful. The ocean could not keep me away from her. I began to change. I saw the need for law, order, and authority. We made love in the park, at her home, in my little room.

"I was in love. We did not argue. For a stretch there was peace and happiness. Then one summer, she stopped seeing me. She told me that I had changed. She saw Russia as it should be—through the eyes of Boris. She had met him in the library. He had introduced her to The First Circle and Cancer Ward.

"It took me a long while to get over Galina. She was beautiful. I was young, immature. I had been false to myself to be true to her. I can't forgive myself. A week ago I met Jasmin. She lives in our apartment building. She is haseen, beautiful. Jasmin is a Muslim girl. I don't care. I have no religion. Jasmin is like Galina."

Yuri too had fallen on his ding-dong. He too would redeem himself.

Vaudeville and Vodka in a Centrifuge

Clearly she has come nigh to me who decks the dark with richest hues:
O Morning, cancel it like debts. [Hymn to Night: Rig-Veda]

My roommate Farooq shut his book with a determined thump and said, "Let's go to the Jama Masjid. We can watch the sunset and feed the pigeons."

I replied, "I will go if Yuri goes. I need protection."

Farooq did not take offense at my immature remark. I had grown up alongside the Muslim minority without feeling that they were alien to us. The only exception was when there was a communal riot somewhere because a Muslim had killed a cow with irreverent and nefarious intent. Then I saw the divide between the Hindu and the Muslim in India. Not that I consider the cow any more sacred than a horse or an elephant. Killing a cow was a symbolic provocation—an act of defiance and disregard. I don't know why these thoughts crossed my mind that day. Perhaps it was because I had been thinking of Jain lying helplessly on a hospital bed and recalling the story of his parents' violent death.

Half an hour later we were at the masjid, leaning against

the concrete railing and watching the sun go down, when Yuri popped the question: "Are you a virgin, Farooq?" Before Farooq could complete his response that seven virgins awaited him in paradise, etc., Yuri was on to this tale about his maternal grandfather who lived in a village outside Prague. He could act, sing, and play the flute. For much of the year he was away from home roaming the country with a theater company. When he did come home after a long tour, he left his wife with yet another child to bear. After the tenth child, Grandma divorced him. She could bear no more. The man was irrepressible. He had his eleventh child with an itinerant actress. Two years later Grandpa came home again in total denial of his divorced state. He did not come alone, repentant and begging for forgiveness.

"No, he was not alone, my grandpa. He brought with him the younger woman and his eleventh child.

"They would all move in with Grandma, a big happy family. Audacity!

"That's when Grandma gave him the final shove."

"What has that got to do with my virginity?" Farooq would not let the important question dangle unanswered.

Yuri ignored him. Yuri was a prolific talker, not a mere pensive scholar.

"Do you know the book of *Corinthians* says, 'It is better to marry than to be aflame with passion'? Grandpa had it both ways. I feel Grandma's pain. I feel my mother's pain. Pain women have to bear. In ancient Judah, if a virgin was violated, the man paid a fine of fifty shekels and married her. If an unmarried woman gave herself to a man, she could be put to death."

One reason for Farooq's devotion to Jain was his commitment to social justice. He had elected to study sociology so he could be an instrument of change. Farooq spoke with his head turned squarely at Yuri.

"I am ashamed to admit in my society women are fenced in within a burqa. It is a form of imprisonment. They get stoned to death in some countries for sex outside of marriage. This day, this age! Unbelievable! My wife will be as free as Milli. Things will change."

I intervened. "When I was at the airport to pick up Milli's mother, I saw a well-dressed, handsome man, middle age I would say, with a neat beard and trimmed moustache. He had the cap on that the sheikhs from the Middle East wear. He had a retinue of women with him. There were seven of them, all bejeweled and wearing burqas. Headscarves concealed a good part of their faces. They chit-chatted and laughed and seemed happy enough. When it came time to head for the taxi or whatever other vehicle the man had arranged …"

"No camels in Delhi," Yuri interjected

Farooq continued. "The man raised his hand and the harem followed like a bunch of school children. I felt sad for the women."

"Singing, 'Let me see what is under the choli [blouse],' and rotating the hip invitingly, Bollywood style, will not solve the world's problem either," interjected Farooq.

Farooq was being defensive. He could be a protagonist and the antagonist on the same topic. He protected his right to say, "I told you so," by being on both sides of the argument. Farooq is colorful. He has many personalities.

Seeing me smile mischievously, and realizing that he had

taken seemingly conflicting views on women's lib, Farooq changed the subject.

He was more persuasive on the next topic. "Six thousand years ago, all issues were tribal. Three thousand years later they were tribal and national. Now all local issues are global in consequence. If there is peace in Bosnia, there is strife in Iran. We will not win. We are in for a rough ride."

Yuri smiled. This was his moment. He pulled a folded sheet of paper from his wallet.

"I have not shown you this before, Gora. You are a poet and this is rotten rice wine compared to what you write ..."

Before he could completely unfold the piece of paper, Farooq grabbed it from Yuri's hand. "What do we have here? A poem! It is titled F-I-S-S-I-O-N" Farooq chuckled.

After he read the first three lines in balladic cadence, his voice became somber. His face lost the mock humor grin. "Let me start again."

In deep elegiac elocution, he began.

Dust charged air
hung heavy—
Dead squirrel smell
dripped
from leaf barren branches
to cracked earth.
Jagged teeth
picked
on charbroiled flesh—
gulped down with heavy water.

Mothers,
eyes delirium sunk,
shrank
from bent limbed babies born.
Nightmare buried fathers
dropped
seeds
tortured
with sick plutonium glow.
Free
Individuals
Speak.
Silence
Is
Ominous.
Nuclear preempt is not a nightmare.

Finishing his recital, Farooq slapped Yuri on his back. "Hot stuff! Gora is a novice compared to you. Gora is in love. He writes soft pudding. This is lava."

I nodded approval. "Nonsense," said Yuri. He became serious and pensive. We remained silent. It was Yuri who spoke again.

"I feel it. This killing and this dying will end. I feel it. Jain will wake one day. I see it. I see it as clear as the sunset and the feathers on the pigeon's back. I see it. I feel it." Yuri's eyes looked beyond the walls of the mosque. Beads of sweat rose on his brow.

Yuri was a scholar. More than that, he was an influence.

He was a dynamo. He permeated the space he was in with the charge, the voltage he carried with him. He would have been a formidable opponent.

What attracted him to India? Was it revulsion for vodka and vaudeville or a premonitory vision that compelled Yuri to leave Russia and be tied inescapably to India? Was this what drew him to Jain? Did he see in Jain an instrument to make the world more peaceful? I saw the beads on his forehead. Tarot cards flashed before my eyes. I relived the tarot card séance.

Clairvoyance

In the beginning there was Self alone ... But He felt no delight ... He then made this self fall in two ... and thence arose husband and wife ... each like half a shell ... He embraced her and men were born. [Brihadaranyaka Upanishad]

On many occasions, Farooq praised Milli. "She is the perfect role model for younger girls."

Yuri would shake his head in agreement. "Milli is fond of tradition and yet receptive to new ideas."

No one is perfect; Milli was superstitious. She believed her lucky number was three and that seven was unlucky.

She manipulated numbers to accommodate her design. If there was a sequence of six and two or say seven and four, she would divide, subtract, add, or multiply till she somehow came up with three in the end. She defended her quest for the comfort number, the rearrangement, as her free will overcoming the external influences of a cosmic phenomena. This idiosyncratic manipulation gave Milli arithmetic latitude beyond the restriction of integral numbers.

"If this is the only conniving you are capable of, you are an honest woman," Milli's mother would interject.

By the end of that summer, the seeds of doubt threatened

my firmly rooted belief in the perfect role model. We were seated on a park bench on a late afternoon, when, out of the blue, she pulled my hands to her lap, held them facing up, twisted and turned them, and gloated over my betrayal of intense surprise. She announced that she had secretly read palmistry all summer long and now considered herself an expert. At first, I played along. If palmistry amused her, I had no reason to be judgmental. But when Milli pulled out a large magnifying glass from her handbag, I saw the big picture.

Placing the magnifier over her palm, she pointed to the figure of eight at the tag end of her fate line. This was absolute proof that she was clairvoyant. A soothsayer in sky-blue salwarkameez, a ponytail of black braided hair, a black dot to the left of her smooth strawberry point chin, is irresistible when holding a large magnifying glass in hand. I decided to go along. Besides, the magnifying glass had exposed my own insecurity. At the moment, I could forgive the entire world if it took to palmistry. I was vulnerable. The figure of eight was convincing proof.

The magnifying glass was back over my palm. My heart line was forked at the end.

"The fork means that you are easily hurt. Just now, you tightened up because I had not let you in on my palmistry lessons."

"Not true," I protested. "I don't believe in this hocus-pocus, that's all."

I saw Milli pout. I became conciliatory. "Okay, tell me if I will be a famous writer. Just curiosity. I don't believe in line reading."

Milli smiled. She was winning. "The Mount of Apollo is

prominent." I wanted to kiss her. I did not have the courage. Besides, we were in a park. There were gawkers. Delhi is not Los Angeles—not yet. Kissing openly in a park in broad daylight is a no-no in New Delhi.

Milli spoke softly. "One day at the hospital I examined Jain's palms."

"Oh! That's what you were doing," I blurted out.

Milli ignored my immature outburst.

"His ring finger is longer than his middle finger—the sign of a visionary."

I nodded in agreement. That point added to palmistry's score!

After a poignant pause, Milli announced, "Jain has the simian line."

She gloated over my puzzlement. "When the head and the heart lines on the palm are merged into one, it is called a simian line. The merger marks a sublime spirit—at least a genius."

"What if he never recovers from coma, Milli? What will the simian line mean then? Falling off a cliff does not require genius!" I regretted that last unkind remark. I wished I could take it back. True, I harbored mixed feelings about Jain. Yet whenever I saw him lying helpless in bed, with little movement to his limbs, I prayed for his recovery and his destined mission.

"What do the lines say about how long Jain will live?" I asked.

Milli took my hand and placed it facing up on her lap.

"Look at your lines. On Jain's hand it is different. The simian line cuts across his life line. So it looks like an asymmetric cross on his palm. What does that say? It says that an obstacle has come across his path. It could end his life. But if he overcomes the hurdle, he will live very, very long."

Milli paused. She placed the magnifying glass over my life line. "See how your life line ends near the crease of your wrist? You will live past eighty. Jain's life line crosses into his wrist."

As I absorbed these revelations, Milli continued in a soft voice, now lower than before. "On his palm, the ends of the simian line and life line diverge widely. That is a sign of recklessness." She paused. "I can't figure that out."

Sohaila

God granted man a boon, "Ask and it will be given."
Man prayed, "Give me the gift that is best for mankind."
"Know Me," God said. "This is best for man." [Upanishad]

To say Sohaila was beautiful would be untrue. A stubby nose and thin lips sat inconspicuously on her heart-shaped face. The fair skin of her small dainty hands loosely clasped in front of her chest contrasted starkly against the black salwar-kameez. Tiny roses were embroidered along the edges of her dupatta. What set Sohaila apart were her deep dark eyes. Kindness spilled out of them as though she constantly felt the pain that dwelled in every heart, the sorrow that welled in every house on the street, and the heavy air that strained through every alley in the city.

Sohaila was a receptionist at Safdarjang Hospital. She issued passes for visitors who came to see relatives or friends admitted to the hospital wards. When she handed Farooq a pass, she apparently accepted Farooq's pass in return. They hit it off from day two—it had taken Farooq that extra day to recover from the shocks of Kalimpong. She was Farooq's steady ever since.

Several weeks after Jain's admission to the hospital, Milli and I accompanied Farooq to pick up Sohaila after her shift ended for the day. It was late afternoon when we reached her counter. Our plan was to go to a movie together. Sohaila had a book open in front of her. The book was about an incident that had happened on a Monday, May 21. We had all seen it on CNN: the stoning to death in Iraq of seventeen-year-old Dua Khalil for her romance with a boy, a Sunni, she being from a different religious sect.

Sohaila was fuming. Anger bolted out of her eyes.

"Few years ago Karzai made rape of a wife not punishable in Afghanistan! This reminds me of another woman in Nigeria who was sentenced to die by stoning. Adultery! To hell with sharia law! They can stone me to death if they hear me."

Her long, pointed fingers curled like a tigress's paw, Sohaila thrust her hands into the air above with determined defiance.

"Can't Muslim women protest as a group?" Milli had asked softly.

We were sitting at corner table at the hospital café where Sohaila could vent her anger without drawing too much attention.

"How?" Sohaila rasped. "Who can fight those who hold the ropes, the wallet, and the guns?"

We did not go to the movie. Sitting instead in the cafeteria, we drank coffee, cup after cup, feeling despondent. Jain was in coma, lying helplessly in a room above. The caffeine could not undo our numbness. Even if Jain recovered, what could one man accomplish? Society was content to let the bullets fly by so long as it did not knock its own wind out. Pervasive narcotic kept the senses of the silent majority anesthetized. The world needed someone—someone higher up.

The Vision

Yajnavalkya spoke thus to Maitreyi, his wife:
It is not for the love of a wife that a wife is dear;
but for the love of the soul in the wife that the wife is dear ...
It is not for the love of religion that religion is dear;
but for the soul of the religion that religion is dear.
[Adapted from the Brihadaranyaka Upanishad]

A month after Milli's revelation that she was a palmist, Yuri and I were on our way back to JNU from another visit to Raj Ghat. Safdarjang Hospital is on the way. We would visit Jain. It was unusually cold for a January afternoon in Delhi.

Inexplicably, the tarot card riddles vexed me like a gnawing toothache. Milli's exposition of Jain's simian line had made the maze more intricate. I was at a loss. I was perplexed at my own frailty. A graduate student at JNU engrossed in the mysteries of Middle Age tarot card predictions and unable to shake off palm line oracles should be subjected to the most intense psychoanalysis.

"You are going mad!" That would be my unwavering verdict if it involved someone else. However hard I tried, I was unable to ignore the tarot card prophesies. My mind was the wrestling ring for two opposing persuasions. Should I fall for the occult mumbo-jumbo? Never! Impossible! Yuri was not incapable of feigning a deceptive swoon. I tried to convince myself that the tarot session histrionics was the masterful act of one possessing Eastern European gypsy instincts. Possibly, it was a Russian's love of histrionics. That was it! But the sweat-soaked bandana? How could I distrust Yuri's sincerity? And the white rose! I confess the mystic fascinated me.

I remembered too Yuri's emphatic "I see it!" and "I feel it!" as we watched the sun set west of Jama Masjid six weeks ago. The intense focus in his eyes! The unswerving voice! The sweat-soaked bandana doused my smoldering suspicions. As dew foresees the coming of day, those beads of sweat foreshadowed a happening. Before my very eyes the white rose was turning to a blood red. Yuri was a scholar. Was this his scholarly vision or subconscious premonitions of a calamity?

In the hallway of Safdarjang we ran into the nurse as she was coming out of Jain's room.

"How is he, sister?" I asked.

"See for yourself," she said as she smiled.

We stared at her back as she walked away. Not once did she turn to relish the astonished curiosity she had set free. We entered Jain's hospital room with the eagerness of a child about to unwrap a gift.

Jain had heard our voices. His head was turned toward the door. His eyes were bright. I had never seen brighter eyes. He looked steadfastly at us. He raised his hands to hold ours. His arm fell back on the bed and he closed his eyes. He was weak.

"The dead will rise" was Farooq's exclamation when I gave him the news on his mobile. He rushed in to witness Jain's surprising recovery. He had been on his way to visit Jain. It was not long after that he was beside Jain's bed, holding his hand and uttering "God is great" over and over.

Milli arrived not long after Farooq. She stood in silence at the foot of Jain's bed. Tears rolled down her cheeks. She tried to keep her face dry, dabbing her eyes with the end of her white handkerchief. Yuri went over to her and put his arm around her.

The nurse came back. She pulled the sheets around Jain so he would be more comfortable. She smiled at us. "You like what you see? The doctors say that he will make quick progress now. Come back in the morning. He needs his rest."

Jain had not spoken a word that evening.

Thereafter, each day brought remarkable progress.

Three evenings later Milli, Yuri, Farooq, and I watched Jain empty half a bowl of soup that the nurse spooned in. The next day he was in a bedside chair wiggling his toes and flexing his feet. Two days later we clapped as Jain shuffled along the parallel bars. Soon he was pushing along thirty feet with a rolling walker.

The doctor predicted a quick recovery. "He will be like before. People in coma from a bad concussion are back to normal amazingly soon."

At the end of that week, Jain was discharged from the hospital. The orderly pushed his wheelchair to the side door where Milli's chauffer waited with her car. Yuri and Farooq helped Jain out of the wheelchair and seated him comfortably in the car. We had confirmed during his illness that Jain had no close relatives living in or near Delhi. A few distant cousins belonging to the Jain or the Kabir family were located. When contacted, they were happy that Jain was under our good care. They never visited or asked about him again. They were not well to do and perhaps were afraid that the cost of Jain's care would be heaped upon them.

An off-duty nurse was hired to care for him in his apartment. The quarters were small but clean and conveniently laid out. The sitting room was the largest, with the kitchen on one end and a bedroom with an adjoining bath at the other. There were very few clothes in the closet—white shirts, khaki trousers, and two navy blue jackets. Books filled the shelves. Two framed photos of two middle-aged couples hung on the wall across from the entrance.

Soon Jain was able to walk without holding on to a walker or to one of us. He fed himself without soiling his kurta. We noticed that he was courting a beard.

Was the mission deleted from his memory when he fell from the cliff? We waited for the day when he would speak to us.

The day came two weeks later. Milli, Yuri, Farooq, and I were spread across Jain's living room one evening. Jain no longer needed a nurse to stay with him round the clock. He sat on a straight-backed chair across from us. He leaned on the Mahatma Gandhi staff I had bought for him when he began to refuse the assistance of a walker. He placed this staff across his knees and began to speak. "As I lay on the mountaintop, my head against a piece of rock, I had a vision."

We sat up, our spines straight as steel rods. Not a word or sound came from us. As Jain broke the expectant silence, these were his next words: "As I lay in apparent unconsciousness, I had a vision."

The words came slowly. We had not heard a single syllable from Jain in months.

This evening his voice was surprisingly clear. He stroked his sprouting beard. Farooq stood up and leaned against the wall six feet from Jain. His eyes were riveted on Jain. As Jain spoke again, a faint smile lit Farooq's face and eyes.

"I had a vision. I had the same vision on three successive days. There is no blur between the images of one day and the next. Each image is imprinted on my mind as carvings on a stone tablet. I see each image as clearly as I see your faces. I remember each word spoken to me."

Jain looked at me. I rose to stand beside Farooq.

"Myths are handed down from father to son, from mother to daughter, through codes carried on our genes from one century to the next. They lie deep within the sleeping mind.

"The memory of past lives lies deep in the well of the unconscious. When I fell from the mountaintop, I was handed a bucket with a rope long enough to ripple the silence of the deep," Jain continued.

"Fifteen hundred years ago, I was a young shepherd in Arabia. I tended a small herd of sheep and goats on the mountains at the edge of Mecca. In the rocky hills of Al Hijaz, finding food is arduous labor for the goats and sheep. Grass and desert plants are sparse. Each day I rose before the sun and led my small flock to the hillside. At the break of dawn one day, as was my habit, I leaned against a rock and watched my flock graze among the rocks. Nearby on a flat bed of rock, a baboon with his flowing mane and long snout courted his four female followers. In the distance I saw a lone ibex high on top of the hill, his white underbelly striped against the dark sky.

As the first red of sunlight lit the animal's long arched horns, I heard footsteps. A holy man in white was climbing the next ridge to a clearing. I moved to a closer vantage point to get a clearer look at him. Once on the next ridge, he sat on rocky ledge. He began writing on what looked like a slate from where I was. I walked back to my herd to be certain that they did not go astray. When I looked up again, the holy man was no longer there. I knew of a cave nearby on the hill. I presumed he was in the cave. I thought no more of him till I saw him descend. He seemed pleased with what he had accomplished."

I felt Milli's right arm on my shoulder. She was standing beside me now. Yuri was standing next to her. I had not heard them move. Jain did not stop speaking. His voice was clear. He was calm. His eyes were as bright as on the first day I had seen him in Kinari Bazaar.

"He came again the following morning. I suspected that he had discovered something valuable inside the cave. He sat outside the cave on the same flat edge of rock as on the morning before. He was bent over the slate again. He appeared to be writing. He did not see me. I moved closer. He was well built. Medium height. His hair and beard were black and curly. From where I stood, I could see he was pleasant and handsome. I went back to my flock. Later, at noon, I found him still bent over the slate. He had not moved. It was past midday when he left. There was no slate in his hand. Perhaps the holy man is writing a new book, I thought. It was not until three years later that I myself learnt to read.

"The hill is called Jabal an-Nur. The cave is well known in

Mecca. On the third day, I waited near the hill, hiding myself behind a large boulder. The holy man had aroused my curiosity. He came before dawn and took the same path toward the cave. I followed him, crouched behind shrubs and rocks. I wanted to see what he did without being seen. The holy man lifted a wooden tablet from behind a rock. The tablet was inscribed with lines of script. I could not see the writing from where I was. I had not learnt to read or write. The holy man placed the tablet on a slab of stone. He brought out a knife from a pocket in his robe. I moved in to get closer. He must have heard my footsteps. He turned around. He saw me. He smiled. His smile was captivating. His eyes were luminous and sincere.

"The holy man asked me to come to him. He placed his hand on my shoulder. He said …"

At this point, Jain gestured that he wanted us to move in closer to him. We moved to within an arm's length of him. He motioned us closer, till our shoulders touched and our heads were crowded over the sitting Jain. He lifted his right hand and touched his forehead. He whispered, "Before the night when words fall from the sky, I will reveal to you what has been revealed to me. We will drink from the same cup in the light of the holy moon."

We did not speak. We knew what he said was true. His eyes were sincere and luminous.

He paused. I moved a step back from where he sat.

What he said next, he said in a loud voice. "A few days later I saw the holy man again. Without sitting a while on the rocks outside, as was his habit, he entered the cave in a hurry. Minutes later he ran down the hill, the tablet held firmly against his chest.

He ran down the hill as if he was chased by a jinni."

"I was afraid he would fall."

Diderot's Prayer

*He unseen passes through illusions that fade
and then is not manifest again. Death and birth
follow naturally—grieve not for the dead.
Wherefore would you grieve for the imperishable?
[Bhagavad-Gita]*

Our past faithlessness had not erupted into outright insurrection. True, we had vacillated between genuine love and devotion to Jain and suspicion as to his stature and true grit. After Jain had whispered the promise of revelation into our ears, we gathered in his apartment each evening to visit, to listen to his wisdom, and to receive our awaited instructions. We were revived by his rebirth. A pile of newspaper cuttings we had saved and bunched together lay in a heap near the leg of the sofa in the corner where Jain sat. He was eager to hear about all that was happening and all that had happened while he was in his deep and prolonged sleep—"meditation" he called it. We read from newspapers and periodicals in turn.

On one such evening, Farooq, on Jain's behest, chronicled the events related to the epidemic of terrorism and religious radicalism over the last decade. Farooq was somber. This touched him more than the rest of us. Yet he was eager. He was pleased that Jain had entrusted this task to him. Milli, Yuri, Sohaila, and I listened as Farooq read his selected excerpts from various newspapers and magazines. Farooq read them without a strict chronologic order. The dire drama of the events was more important to Farooq than the year of their occurrence.

"New Delhi: The sun beat on the tar with red-hot hammers. School was over early because of the oppressive heat. Outside the school, children waited for their bus to arrive; even the most playful stood quietly. Their bare heads shielded inadequately with notebooks, they shifted their feet from time to time as the tar softened to a hot stickiness under their shoes. The summer sun is cruel in New Delhi. The sun can burn the sky.

"Baghdad: Thirteenth of July, 1,800 miles west of Delhi, US soldiers from the third infantry division were engaged in a "cordon and search" mission. The brutal Baghdad sun reflected off the armored Humvees. Ten-year-old Mustafa approached the flak-jacketed soldier in the lead vehicle to beg for a handful of US candy.

"Back in Delhi, the school children gathered their belongings. They had seen the bus turn the corner. Relief was in sight. The bus would be hot, but they would have a roof over their heads.

"The children scurried to get ahead in line as the bus came within fifty feet of the school gate. A child fell. His sandals had become glued to the molten tar. Other children laughed at his predicament. The bus had now come to a stop. The bus driver opened the door to let the children in.

"In Baghdad, the soldier shooed the children away. 'Go home.'

"It was not safe to be near a Humvee. The soldier wiped his

brow. Mustafa and his friends would not leave without a piece of American candy.

"'Go away, go away.' But even as he said it, the soldier dug into his pocket and pulled out a handful of candy.

"Back in Delhi, as soon as the bus door opened, children rushed to climb in. As the boys scrambled in and the fallen child recovered his sandal, a loud explosion lifted the rear of the bus. Its tires shredded, the bus jolted to the ground with a violent thud. It tilted to the right in an ominous slant. Debris flew out of the shattered windows—books, metal, glass, limbs, and ash.

"The flak-jacketed soldier dropped the handful of candies to the ground. He had spotted the SUV veering around the corner. It sped past the cordon. Before he could shoot out its tires, the SUV exploded and scattered its misery around the parked Humvee. Mustafa lay on the road near the dead soldier, his outstretched hand barely touching a fallen candy.

"'Their bodies are tender,' said a man as he lifted a wounded child in his arms. 'Just the force of an explosion hurts them.'

"Egypt: 1:15 a.m. One week later. Three car bombs exploded in a mad succession and tore the nocturnal soft cover of the sea. Over the austral tip of the Sinai Peninsula where the Red Sea embraces it with two extended arms, the sky was on fire. The shattered front wall of the Gazala Gardens Hotel exposed its vulnerable core. The rock music stopped. Two bodies lay in front of the hotel gate, face down in ultimate surrender.

What were their last thoughts, their last words? Did they know each other? Were they lovers? These thoughts occurred to me.

"Near them lay a severed head. A red-stained babushka

clung to the woman's chin." Farooq continued to read.

"London: July 2005. A series of coordinated suicide attacks on the London's public transport system during the morning rush hour ... were carried out by four British Muslim men. Three were of Pakistani and one of Jamaican descent ... Fifty-two people were killed and around seven hundred were injured ... They were apparently motivated by British involvement in the Iraq War.

"Kabul: March 4, 2006. American Marines reacted to a bomb ambush with excessive force in eastern Afghanistan, killing twelve civilians. In May 2007, a formal apology was offered."

His voice grim and low, Farooq continued after a long somber silence. He said, "I am going to read excerpts from *The New York Times* next."

Jain sat in his chair, leaning on his staff.

"Mumbai: November 30, 2008. The attacks, which began on 26 November and lasted until 29 November, killed at least 173 people ... The attacks drew widespread condemnation across the world ... Ajmal Amir Kasab, the only attacker who was captured alive, disclosed that the attackers were members of Lashkar-e-Taiba ...

"If you are a young Muslim male looking for training in jihad, Pakistan is where you are likely to find the opportunity." Farooq read from *The Wall Street Journal*.

"The opportunity is everywhere," Yuri interjected. "Look at Chechnya."

"Look at India. We have had three Muslim presidents. Yet LaskareTaiba terrorizes Kashmir and launches a cruel attack on

Mumbai. We belonged to the same country for ages." Milli was furious.

"In the past, Jaish-e-Mohammad has claimed credit for the death of scores of Indian Soldiers in Kashmir!" I interjected. "Credit for killing? What have we become? Regressed into a horde of savage hunters? If religion is the mother's milk of politics, we are all being poisoned."

"Without hope, without fear," Yuri mused.

"When fear eases, there is hope, and action. Action brings change."

Jain had spoken with his usual soft forcefulness. I remembered the man rescuing a young boy from a hungry crowd. I remembered the mountain. I remembered his whispered words.

Farooq stopped. He turned the pages he was holding. A single drop of tear shone on his right cheek. He made no attempt to wipe the tear. His voice was somber as before. He continued.

"During holy Ramadan, two blasts on one day! In Kabul the Taliban attacked the British Cultural Centre to celebrate 1919 when British rule of Afghanistan ended. Eight people died in the attack. On the same day forty-three people were killed in a bomb attack on a mosque in northwestern Pakistan. 'I saw bodies ... everywhere,' an observer said."

Yuri interrupted Farooq.

"I recall the Cordova imam asked in New York, 'What would Jesus do?' Imams want tolerance everywhere except where sharia is the law. What hypocrisy! But let us not forget Oslo."

Jain put his hand on Yuri's shoulder and smiled. Yuri stopped.

"There is no need to read more. I too have read. Paris. London. Nigeria. Cairo. Amsterdam. Needless violence everywhere. You have done well in presenting the problem." He thanked Farooq as he embraced him.

Jain told us, "When the enemy is within, change must come from within."

Saying this, Jain put his cane aside and knelt, hands folded on his chest. Farooq, Sohaila, Yuri, Milli, and I too got down on our knees. We faced Jain as he prepared to pray.

"Remember Diderot's prayer, Gora? O God, I do not know if you exist. I ask nothing in this world, for the course of events is determined by its own necessity if you do not exist, or by your decree if you do … here I stand, as I am, a necessarily organized part of eternal and necessary matter—or perhaps your own creation …"

"Let us pray," he said.

He bowed his head farther without touching the ground with his forehead. We repeated these words after Jain:

God made you and me and all that walk or stand.
God made us with planet dust and His breath.
God's breath is His psalm.
God's epic is the universe.
Hear the voice of the planets—
Who can silence the psalm? God is reason.

Reason is God. Man, bold in starlight,
sings the song of the planets,
His song.

He created the sun so I can see,
the night so I can reflect,
silence so I can hear,
reason so I can find
the path though the wilderness.
Fill me with love, O God; in love I will find action.

Jain stood up, touched our foreheads in turn with his right hand, and blessed each one of us. "Read *The Passages*," he said. He kissed each one of us in turn on our forehead and turned and left the room.

Milli whispered, "He draws me like a magnet. But what did he mean, read *The Passages*?"

Struck with awe, Farooq mumbled, "It is like being in a warm undercurrent, challenging and frightening."

I shouted after Jain, "What does it mean? What are you asking us to do?"

Jain turned back. He smiled. "You will carry on what I will put in action. You will carry on and spread the message."

Yuri said, "Let us find eight more."

Before the Cock Crows

Speak no more!
Thou turnst mine eyes into my very soul
And there I see such black and grained spots
As will not leave their tinct. [William Shakespeare: Hamlet]

Once outside the building that housed Jain's apartment, Yuri spoke first. "Which one of us will disown him before the cock crows thrice?"

Let us find eight more! The cock's crow! Yuri's references revealed the depth of his belief in Jain. Our mission, still a sketch, not a blueprint, would begin that night if Jain told us what he precisely wanted us to do. We were prepared. Were we drawn to Jain because of his charisma? His courage? His mission to bring change?

"Like you, Gora, I feel the presence of greatness when around him. I feel something breathtaking is about to happen. But I am human." Yuri acknowledged his doubts.

"He has a plan, he should reveal it to us," Farooq complained.

"Yes," I keyed in. "Why does Jain assume that we will all follow his lead without revealing what exactly is expected of us?"

"'Read *The Passages*,' he says. Muttering philosophy is not the mantra for insurrection," Farooq protested again.

"Every action begins with love," Jain had said during one of his lectures.

"Even murder?" someone in our class had challenged.

"Every action begins with love," Jain reiterated.

"Love is the desire to associate with another kindred soul or an object. He who loves knowledge and seeks it associates with a book. If you love a woman, you search for her, to be with her. He who loves life and wants to heal its blemishes becomes a doctor. Love is the driving force for the associations. Malevolence is inaction or perverse reaction to another action. Murder is a reaction not action. Love is proactive."

Farooq had signed with his hand. "What is he saying?" I had not fully grasped the logic of Jain's assertion either. Yuri, the savant, had shaken his head and said, "Makes sense. Good is action, evil reaction. God is action, the devil reaction. You see, Gora, he is drawing a moral line. Being constructive is action, being destructive is reaction. By defining action as love, we deter the destructive trait that is in all of us."

"Words will fall from the sky. He said it. He has never disappointed us." It was Milli who had the last word as we parted that night and headed home—Milli to her house, we back to our dorm.

Milli was right. Jain would never disappoint us. In my heart I too believed this as much as I grumbled because of the lack of clarity. He had risen from the dead—in Farooq Shahjehan's words. Jain was the light—without him the world and our lives would be shut out in darkness.

The Passages

Sohaila was not familiar with *Passages.* It was a pamphlet Jain distributed to each student who attended his lecture series Snakes and Ladders. We had read through the compilation during the semesters. The pamphlet did not include any of Jain's

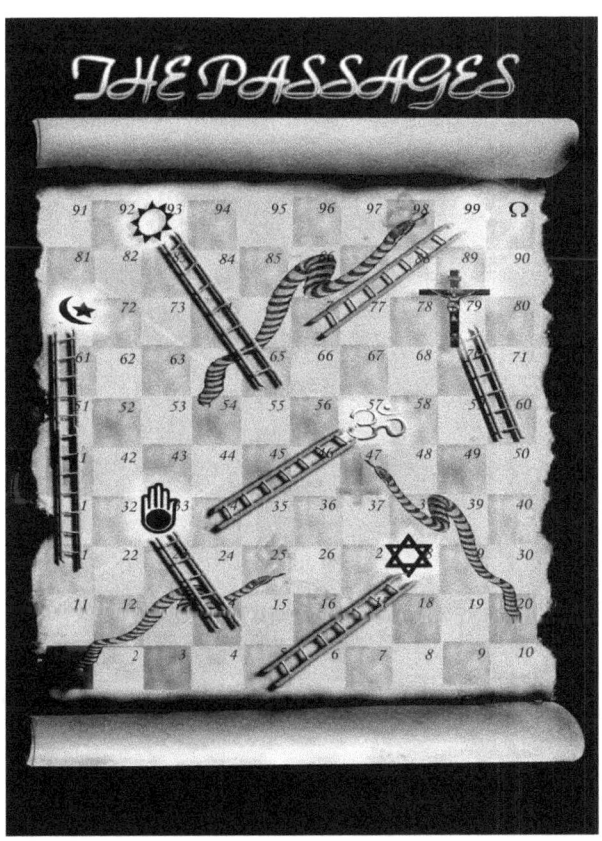

lecture topics or his comments. It contained quotes from various sacred texts. Jain's preference for one over another was not disclosed. In keeping with his theme, Snakes and Ladders, the cover page of the pamphlet had a rather intriguing illustration. There was another remarkable aspect to the pamphlet. It included quotations from several poets. Placing the poet on the pedestal of philosophers!

We read *Passages* again. We did not find a message in it that guided us to a specific plan or a preordained path.

"Why can't he just tell us?" Farooq was frustrated.

"The words will fall to us from the sky. Did he not say so? Be patient, Farooq." Milli was staunch in her faith.

"Likely he is still working on the plan. Before his illness he told us about a tycoon and other influential people he had met. It has only been three months since he recovered from the coma," she reminded us.

I gave Sohaila a copy of the first two pages of the pamphlet.

I am the source and the end.
I am the evolution,
the energy that drives the wind of change
and the stillness over the lake. [Bhagavad-Gita]

Will is the man. [John Wilson, *Noctes Ambrosianae*]
Die when you will, you need not wear
At Heaven's court a form more fair
Than Beauty here on earth has given. [Thomas Moore]

For they breathe truth that breathe their words in pain.
*[*William Shakespeare, *Richard II]*

*The true medicine of the mind is philosophy. [*Cicero*]*
*Cause and effect are two sides of one fact. [*Ralph Waldo Emerson, *Essays]*
*Philosophy is common-sense in a dress suit. [*Oliver S. Braston, *Philosophy]*
*The Rational is the Real and the Real Rational. [*Hegel*]*
Reading furnishes our mind only with materials of knowledge; it is thinking makes what we read ours. *[*John Locke, *Conduct of Understanding]*

*God builds his temple in the heart on the ruins of churches and religions. [*Ralph Waldo Emerson, *Conduct of Life, Worship]*

What religion is he of? Why, he is an Anythingarian. *[*Jonathan Swift, *Polite Conversation]*

*Consider the lilies of the field, how they grow ... even Solomon in his glory was not clothed as one of these ... Beware of the false prophets, who come to you in sheep's clothing, but inwardly are ravenous wolves. You will know them by their fruits. Are grapes gathered from thorns? [*From the *Bible: Sermon on the Mount]*

Jesus took Peter, James and John to the high mountains. As the men watched, Jesus's appearance changed

> so that his face shone like the sun, and his clothing became dazzling white. Suddenly Moses and Elijah appeared and began talking with Jesus...The disciples were terrified and fell face down on the ground ...As they descended from the mountain, Jesus commanded them, 'Do not tell anyone of this, until I have risen from the dead.' [Gospel of Matthew]

> "Give to Caesar what is Caesar's and to God what is God's." [Gospel of Mark]

Asked why he and his disciples spent time with sinners, Jesus replied, "It is not the healthy who need a physician, the sick do. I have come to call on sinners to turn them from sin." [Adapted from *Gospel of Luke*, a gentile physician]

> Mankind was once one community. Then God sent forth prophets ...In the name of God, the compassionate, the merciful ... It is He who makes the lightning flash upon you, inspiring you with fear and hope, and gathers up the heavy clouds. The thunder sounds his praises ... He hurls his thunderbolt at whom He pleases. Yet the unbelievers wrangle about God. [Koran]

> The first noble truth: Life is dukkha [grief]
> The second noble truth: Cause of dukkha is craving.
> The third noble truth: Detachment from craving transcends dukkha.
> The forth noble truth: Now hear this: The Noble Eight-

The Last Day of Ramadan

fold Path leads to the cessation of dukkha—Right understanding, Right thought, Right speech, Right action, Right livelihood, Right effort, Right mindfulness, Right concentration. [Sermon of Buddha]

But as for me, I came so close to the edge of the cliff!
My feet slipping, and I near death ...
Mountains rose and valleys sank
to the level you decreed ...
You sent rain on the mountains
from your heavenly home
and filled the earth with the fruits of your labor.
I will not die, but I will live
to tell what the Lord has done.
A mortal ripens like seed
and like seed is born again.

It is God who has made the earth a dwelling place
for you, and the sky its ceiling.
The light of the moon!
The four gates yet only One.
  [An amalgamation from the *Bible*, *Koran*, *Zen Buddhism*, and *Upanishad*]

Rebirth

Yahweh advances like a hero,
His fury is stirred like a warrior's.
He gives the war shout, raises hue and cry,
Marches valiantly against his foes. [2, Isaiah]

I did not allude to Milli's clairvoyance—and to her idiosyncrasies—to cast doubt on her intelligence or to detract from her suitability as a role model. I was intrigued by Milli's interpretation that Jain's palm betrayed recklessness, thus far an unsuspected trait. Jain's actions revealed courage. He was outspoken. To me, at least, his actions betrayed no trace of recklessness. I respected Milli's intuitive powers. I would not ignore her. I chalked up her interpretation of the lines on Jain's palm to the error inherent to palmistry and apprehension for a loved one, which can often muddle the brain.

Much to my dismay however, her deduction that Jain had a reckless trait found support when Jain resumed lecturing again at JNU not long after the prayer session at his apartment. Bewildering events unfolded from that day on. Milli sat next to me in class that first day when Jain returned to lecture. It was the second week of April.

"I told you, Gora, he will return. You never take my words seriously," she said. Jain had not prepared us at all for the transformation. I was confused. All I could say in reply was, "I will keep my faith in Jain." I tried desperately to ignore the simian line across Jain's palm that flashed ominously on my radar screen. During these moments of desperation, I took refuge in his whispered words—words that he had revealed while leaning on the staff I had presented him.

The main reason for our consternation was the change in Jain's attire. When he lectured at JNU before the accident in the mountains, an immaculately clean white shirt and well-pressed khaki trousers, were Jain's invariable choice. Throw a blue jacket around his shoulders when it was cold—never otherwise. Even on social occasions we never saw Jain in traditional Muslim garb. On the first day back to teaching after his trial in the mountains, Jain shocked everyone in class with his new attire: a traditional Arabic styled disdasha, a white kaftan reaching below his knees.

"The black turban signifies that he is a descendent of the Prophet Muhammad," Farooq whispered into my ears.

That day after class, I asked Jain, "Do you believe in rebirth?" I was sarcastic.

Jain spun a sermon. "Christians believe in the Day of Judgment—a one-time rebirth. Islam speaks of the last trumpet call when the dead will rise before Allah's throne and hear of their eternal prize or punishment. The Hindu believes in Darwinian rebirth—evolution of many births based on karma."

Then he looked at me. It was a strange look. It was full of love, and yet he was admonishing me with that look. "Is not my coming back to life rebirth? There is life beyond this one, Gora. There is no fear of death if you believe in eternal life, Gora. You can be reborn in one lifetime, Gora."

Jain had addressed me by my name three times. I felt the way Peter must have felt about Jesus.

I remember very little else of what Professor Jain had taught during that class. I was so taken aback by his change of garb. The four gospels record the teachings of Jesus with such likeness of words and phrases. All I can recall is that he had mentioned the four of us by name during that lecture, and that he spoke of matter and soul being the same, and that he spoke of victory.

Elsewhere

The demon of angry arrogance struts with peacock's self-conceit—to forfeit eternity for a glimpse of fame and paradise for a moment's gain. [Bhagavad-Gita]

On several occasions before his accident and after his recovery, Mr. Jain had told us of his contact with a tycoon. He had not mentioned his full name but called him "a Mr. Z." Later after August 29, we learnt more about the tycoon, his life, and the problems facing his family, from press reports of interviews with the tycoon and his confidant, Syed Musa, and from his daughter-in-law, Janice, who came alone to the dedication ceremony of the Assembly Hall on the fourth anniversary of August 29 and made a donation to it. Over some objection, I had accepted the check.

Various anecdotes pieced together told Mr. Z's story.

Mr. Zakiruddin's computer hardware manufacturing and distribution operations had mapped a triangle with Mumbai, Delhi, and Kolkata at the apices. Nine years ago, BU, his company, had expanded its operation to Dubai—four points on a quadrangle. Mr. Z looked every bit a tycoon.

On a particular day toward the end of spring, Mr. Zakiruddin stood at the side entrance to the corporate office, ready to board his helicopter. The helipad was a hundred feet away. After he extinguished a half-smoked cigar against a sandbox near the door, Mr. Zakiruddin tugged on the collar of his loose-fitting khaki bush shirt and stretched his legs. Locating his head offices at Gaziabad had been an astute move. On another day, Mr. Zakiruddin would scan the complex through his rimless gold spectacles and gloat over his industrial success. Today he waited impatiently for the chopper to be ready for take-off. As the rotors revved up and the grass on the lawn changed shades from green to gray and then to green again, the tycoon lowered his head and stepped toward the chopper. A young man dressed in white followed Mr. Z. He clutched the businessman's briefcase tightly as he ascended to the helicopter.

Protecting his long hair in the cup of his two large square hands, the tycoon hurried toward the helicopter. The insignia painted on the belly of the heli—a soft crescent silver moon holding a mellow orange sun—would on another day bring a smug smile on Mr. Z's sun-burnt face. Today his tired eyes avoided the sign. At the end of a turbulent day, a worried Mr. Z was going home.

Once seated inside the helicopter, Mr. Zakiruddin frowned. Janice had called from Chicago. What he heard from her was disturbing. He would have to find a solution. He would never sleep peacefully otherwise.

Twelve years ago, his son completed his MBA at Northwestern in Chicago. On graduation day, seated on a bench by the lake, the young Muslim tipped his square-topped black hat and proposed marriage to Janice, an Irish Catholic classmate, the daughter of his political science professor. Over the sounds of dashing waves on the eastern perimeter of the university campus, Janice accepted. He was charming, witty, and outgoing. Janice did not resist. Three months later, Mr. Zakiruddin blessed the marriage. The couple settled in Evanston. They were happy.

Then came September 11, 2001! Everything changed. Neighbors began to avoid the couple. They felt as though they were social outcasts.

A year later, Mr. Z was blessed with a grandson, Ali.

Things would get better once 9/11 faded from people's mind, they comforted each other. But people's attitude to 9/11 did not change. It grew stronger. Events in and out of the United States kept the memory burning as fiercely as the first awful day—the images of dust clouds, the crumbling buildings, the people running scared, and people rushing to help. Mr. Z asked them to move to London so the son could oversee Mr. Z's business in the Middle East.

"Move closer to me, closer to India. It takes seven hours to fly from London to Delhi, almost an entire day from Chicago. I must see Ali once a month. You start packing. You will love it in London. I won't ask you to move to Dubai. Janice may not be happy there," Mr. Z told his son.

Janice and her husband needed little coaxing. They were relieved. They moved to London in the winter of 2003.

Life was happy and placid for a while. Ali was in school. Janice kept busy with family and a part-time job at a law firm. On occasion she would accompany her husband on his frequent flights among London, Dubai, and Delhi. Nothing made Mr. Z happier than bouncing Ali on his shoulders. Mr. Z said, "You are going to be a king, the king of all people, the whole world. People will bow before you."

Then came 2005 and the London bombings. Their life was unsettled again. Ali was three. For the next two years, life was tense for the young family, but nurturing Ali as he grew up in London, and the frequent business trips, kept them occupied. They were detached from the events—the shocks and aftershocks as extremists hammered the foundation of civil society.

One day Ali came home from school and broke into unrelenting tears. His friends refused to play with him. "'Your dad's a terrorist,' they told me. 'He makes bombs in his basement.'"

Janice talked to the school principal the very next day. She was assured the situation would ease with the passage of time. Children were given lessons on diversity. They printed children of various races, creeds, colors, and ethnicities dancing on the globe on United Nations greeting cards. Kids can carry a cruel stick. Years went by, but the boy still suffered. He had few friends. He was a sensitive boy. The psychiatrist had said that in time the boy would be fine.

Mr. Z pursed his lips. He rubbed the tip of his left thumb against the center of his forehead. He was worried about the boy. The boy was his life.

Several years passed. Nothing changed. Janice called the other day to say that she was considering moving to India. Her husband was against the move—giving in to prejudice was cowardly. He would not teach his son to run and hide.

Janice was adamant. "I will not raise my son where every day he feels like an alien."

Mr. Z remembered a business associate, who was also a cousin, say once, "The West is after us. Do you really believe that it was suicide bombing that destroyed the business district of Karachi? It was a planned attempt to cripple Pakistan's economy. Mark my word: India will be next."

Mr. Zakiruddin lit another cigar. Mr. Z loved his son, though his son's lack of the fighting spirit made him uneasy. Ali would be different. Mr. Zakiruddin had to act. Alienation was fencing in his son's family. He had to liberate them.

Mr. Z leaned back on his seat. His bushy eyebrows glowed as he puffed on the cigar. His face began to relax. He wrote on a notepad as he spoke to the young man in white clutching his briefcase.

"As soon as we are home, get the security chief at our Dubai office on the phone. He is Egyptian. He speaks fluent English. His name is Syed Musa. Tell him to catch a flight to Delhi. Waste no time. The sooner he gets here, the better. This is urgent. Arrange for his stay in Delhi. He will be here awhile."

SM was the right man. He had been on the mark in Dubai. Planning and execution—that was business in a nutshell. This situation with Ali was far more important than business. Mr. Z would go as far as was needed. He had heard rumblings about discourses at JNU. Not much happened in Delhi that escaped the ears of the tycoon.

A brave young man was teaching openly for change at JNU. In a god-fearing society that accepts change slowly, a society eager to light a funeral pyre for an iconoclast while playing western music in the background, anything could happen.

Mr. Z lifted his left thumb to his forehead.

Mr. Z was a devout Muslim. He visited the masjid often. Allah had given him so much. He prayed five times a day—the Nawaz was the most important duty in a man's life. His empire had flourished because he was a believer. Mr. Z recited his prayers without fail—whether he was in Delhi, Chicago, or London—in a mosque, at home, or in the aisle next to his first-class plane seat. On this aspect of his life, Mr. Z would not compromise.

The tycoon knelt beside his helicopter seat. He touched his ears. He bent down till his head touched the floor. The vibration was unpleasant. Mr. Z pushed his head down farther, forcefully against the shudder of the copter floor. He would be firm, unwavering, and relentless. He prayed.

Nephilim—Giant from the Sky

Before I formed you in the womb I knew you,
And before you were born I set you apart. [Old Testament: Jeremiah]

Jain did not return to his accustomed dress code—khaki trousers and a white shirt—after that first day back at JNU in his newfound Muslim garb. He kept the beard as well—soon it grew long, black, and curled. We understood. It was a symbolic act. My intuition told me that the change of garb was a clue to Jain's next planned move. What was Jain planning? Was the tycoon in his plan? Jain had said the tycoon was bigoted. He has met some other influential men and women, he had said. He had met some clerics, he had told us. We felt something big was about to happen. But what? Even Yuri could not figure this out. I had a role in whatever it was that was about to happen. I did not know what part I would be asked to play. None of us could guess the cast in the drama. But one thing was certain: the transfiguration had begun.

In the days that followed, Jain regained his usual vigor. However one change was noticeable: periods of energized activity or speech were punctuated by moments when he was lost to his environment in apparent deep thought. Henceforth we met often in Jain's apartment. Each day we expected him to reveal more of his plan, our mission, to us, his disciples. He revealed bits at a time but not the details of his plan of action. I guessed from his words that he was on his way to executing his action soon.

"The time has come for radical change in the way we think."

He spoke of courage. He spoke repeatedly about the sanctity of life, how precious it was.

"God is aware of each of his children, Gora. The waste of a single life brings pain to God."

One evening toward the end of April, at Jain's apartment, Yuri said this: "We are with you. We will be there when you need us. Tell us how we should prepare ourselves." Jain reminded Yuri of the parable of the rich man and the servant entrusted in the care of the house when the master went on a journey. Jain was fond of the parables in the gospels.

That evening, Jain announced that he would be away for two weeks. When asked who he was to meet, he said, "Some people crucial to our mission. I have to convince them that our goal is worthy of dramatic change in the way we think about religious texts."

When we asked where he was going, he said mystically, "I am always with you. Prepare the mind. When trained, the mind can do whatever it chooses to do. Learn how to spread messages quickly and effectively."

This was a difficult period for all of us. As much as Jain drew us together as a giant magnet would chunks of iron, our minds strayed because of the lack of clear directions. We wanted Jain to tell us what our individual roles would be in the coming action. What was the action to be? What form would it take? Civil disobedience? Fasting unto death? Futile immolation by the fire as did the Buddhist priests in Indochina?

At last we had one lead to follow. Spreading his message! Blogs, Facebook? We became adept at all the available social media. We suspected that Jain was preparing himself as much as he was preparing us.

It was hot day early in June. I rushed into his class. I was a bit late. Farooq had kept a book on the seat next to him. I sat down in it as Jain was about to begin his lecture. He appeared gaunt.

Jain began the class saying, "I am going to read to you a poem Gora shared with me a few months back."

I looked at Farooq. He smiled and nodded in approval.

Which poem would he read? I had shared several with Jain since his classes began. Not the one on Brahma that I had read to Milli at the library doorsteps! Milli was sitting behind us. I did not turn back to look.

As Jain began to read the poem, I remembered that I wrote it after a series of gruesome events had spread over the globe over the past year. They left me with the conviction that the dismal state of world affairs would never be mended, and that when posterity dug us out of a volcanic eruption that smothered us in ash and dust and debris, they would certainly find us choking each other by the throat, our bayonets bare, clutching AK rifles as if they were our most prized love.

Who was it that said "man was molded after His image"? "Not one hemlock's grain worth of Socratic logic there" was Yuri's stance on the topic.

Jain read the poem, his voice deep and resonant as if it came from behind clouds:

We deer-stare each other—

Who will take
the first step
across the boundary?

our lives,
livelihood

held in check
at the point of a gun
at the checkpoint—
Who will cross the divide—
take the first step
across the boundary?

"*Wall Street Journal*, March 29, 2009: As Obama outlines Afghan strategy, blast near border rattles Pakistan. 'In a grim reminder of the threat facing the two countries, a suicide bombing leveled a packed mosque Friday near Pakistan's tribal areas, killing at least fifty people in a region where Islamic militants have put up fierce resistance to a Pakistani army offensive.'"

Jain read the excerpt. He continued. "That happened years ago. Some of you may not recall the details. Layers of similar incidents have piled on each other, obscuring the memory of the old. Politics survives on the faded memory of the people.

"This is politics. You will ask what this *New York Times* story has to do with philosophy and religion. Everything, I say.

Religion is politics. It always was politics. I have nothing against politics and politicians. They serve their role in society. I do take a stand against whitewashing over a false graffiti. Change must come. We must forget the violence condoned by past religions in the name of God. We must, as modern societies, sieve the good in religious text from the bad—'holy amnesia,' as some have called it. The whitewash over false scripts washes off in the rain. False praise of a false position perpetuates misconceived use of tenets—even those which have gone unchallenged for ages.

"Why else would a group in Pakistan blow up a mosque a few months earlier? It is one Muslim against another—Sunni against Shia, and both against the rest of the world. If that is religion, religion is politics.

"Remember al-Awlaki, the Muslim cleric born in USA. A few years back, he purportedly called for jihad against the country where he was born—in the name of Islam! He hopes to make jihad as American as apple pie and as British as afternoon tea. According to US intelligence, his influence over English-speaking Muslims is considerable. He is hero to them! This is the time for change. It is here. It is here now. We must not wait.

"I remember my mother saying, 'There is so much sadness in life. Who knows if God cares?' God is a computer with infinite memory. He knows, He remembers, He keeps score, neither sad nor happy at what living beings do.

"God cares. When you look deep into the night sky, you know God cares."

This day was the end of a semester. At the end of the session, we met with Jain in his campus office.

"Do not lose heart no matter how long I am away. When

all the preparations are made for our mission, I will send you word."

"Where will you be? Milli asked.

Jain remained silent for a moment. Handing me the key to his flat, he said to us, "Do not lose faith. Look for me in the sky."

This day was the last we saw him at JNU. The administration office later confirmed that Professor Jain had resigned.

We were on alert.

The mission had begun. It would be many days before we were to see Jain again.

The Digital Image

When our revelations are recited to them, clear as they are, the unbelievers say: This is sorcery. Such is their description of the truth when it is declared to them. [Koran 46:7]

From that day, we went to check Jain's apartment each day—twice on some days. On each visit, we opened the door to his apartment anxiously, eager to see if he had returned. Each day we found his toothbrush in the same cradle, the soap untouched in the dish, the bed unslept in. The books on the shelf remained in the same order. Though Jain did not tell us when we would see him again or where he would be in the coming days, we did not stop searching for Jain. The building fees had been paid in advance for a year. We opened the windows to let the sun shine in and left dejected after we closed them before we departed each day.

Several weeks after Jain's disappearance from JNU, I was witness to this curious incident. It was a holiday. The morning sun was still mellow. The traffic was light. Milli had gone out of Delhi to visit an aunt. Unable to shake Jain off my mind, I went for a walk with no particular destination in mind. Between short bus rides and pedestrian meandering, I rambled through the town pointing my palm-sized Nikon Digital, a birthday gift from Milli, at everything that appeared of interest. I was alone.

I was across the back road from Jama Masjid when, through the lens, I saw a man in a black ankle-length kaftan leaning against the back wall of the great masjid. I moved across surreptitiously toward the front of the building, keeping a safe distance. There were a few people entering and exiting the mosque on the flight of sandstone steps up front and through the arched entrance. Feeling safer, I moved back toward the back of the mosque again, trying to stay behind trees and shrubs when I could.

I took a closer look at the man in the black kaftan. Through the zoom I could see his attire more clearly. A white and blue striped scarf concealed most of his face and neck. Only his eyes showed through. Two cartridge magazines marked his chest with a menacing X. He spotted me as I shot the frame. His left hand grabbed the barrel of his AK-47. He swung his weapon. The barrel was pointed at me as he ran toward me. I lunged to the ground behind a shrub. I covered my head with my arms and waited for a barrage of bullets. I heard no shots. When I rose and looked in the direction of the mosque, the man in the black kaftan was no longer there. The mosque was known to have guards.

A fortnight later I came back to the mosque. I was alone. I admit I was a trifle scared. On the square upper level of the masjid, I saw the man in black again. I confess I was not certain it was he. Of his anatomy, I had only seen his eyes and that through a camera. As I watched the pigeons pick off grains from the expansive square of the Jama Masjid, I studied the man in the black kaftan—same height, same build as the man in my digital Nikon. From the boundary wall where I stood, he was sixty feet away. Though he held no AK47 this time, I was convinced that he was the same man I had photographed. If he had spotted me too, I was unaware. What I observed was his repeated glancing toward the prayer room. He was waiting for someone to come out of the room, I thought.

I kept a careful eye on him. I had not forgotten the artillery. To avoid being obvious, I feigned interest elsewhere in the compound and its surrounding. Because of my pretended nonchalance, I had neglected my watch longer than intended. Minutes later, drawn by the sound of pigeon wings flapping and scattering husk and downy feathers in a conical whirl, I looked in his direction again. I saw the man in the black kaftan take quick steps toward the main prayer room where a second man had appeared. Though he was half hidden by the door, and in spite of the distance, I could swear that this second man in white kaftan was Jain. I rushed to the door.

I shouted, "I want to speak to you! When will we see you again?"

The dust, the flying husk, and the pigeons that took off again slowed my run. When I arrived at the door and looked through it, I found the prayer hall empty. I saw no one. I cursed in exasperation. As I walked back listlessly toward the hostel, more doubts clouded my mind. Was it really Jain? Had I made a fool of myself shouting after an unknown man? The man did wear a beard—a beard can camouflage the familiar.

On those days of Jain's absence, Milli, Yuri, Farooq, and I met most evenings at either Jain's apartment or at Milli's bungalow. More than just friends, we were tied together by fate. We searched desperately for clues. We wanted to understand Jain as much as we wanted a clue to his plans.

"Take up a cross," Yuri said. "Let us prepare to follow Jain bearing it along Janpath, bruised and beaten, struggling towards the Parliament!"

Jain was not planning an attack on anyone or anything. Of that we were certain. That would violate his ethos. Why did he resign from JNU? He had a ready pulpit from which he could spread his own message.

Farooq, Yuri, Milli, and I were walking the wilderness—for far more than forty days and forty nights. Yes, man does not live by bread alone.

I recalled a playwright's one-line parody of Shakespeare—something to the effect that all the world is a stage, and most players are dreadfully unprepared.

Ijtihad in a Cauldron

Nothing exists except atoms and empty space; everything else is opinion. [Democritus: Greek philosopher, fifth century BCE]

The tarot card séance, the simian line on Jain's palm, his disappearance, the vision of him near the masjid prayer hall—all this placed my brain in a state of red alert. My emotions hit high and low notes at random. The discordant strains made maddening sense. I was all over the globe picking up the fallen carcass of human tragedy.

Darfur was a tormenting replay of Biafra. Baghdad looked more and more like Saigon in the desert. More peaceful in 2010 admittedly, but would the regime last? Chaos plagued the western border of Pakistan. The pope's quotation of history had angered Muslims. Sulfurous fumes—to a particular faction—hung over the chamber of the United Nations in New York. The United States was attempting to reclaim the high moral ground after being soiled in the grimy oil pits. Americans in large numbers doubted that Obama was a Christian. The world was in a witch's brew.

The United States was bogged down by a recession, Barak Obama's potential promise was now a gaping doubt, and his periphrastic fireworks were cacophonies within an empty vessel. Verbal mortar was being lobbed across the India-Pakistan border. Suicide bombers groped the world in search of a lottery ticket to paradise.

"It is not human need but human greed." I could not silence those words knocking on my drums like the bark of street dogs tearing the silent veil of midnight. I was in a state of frenzy and Milli knew it.

We were on the verandah of Milli's house. Milli stretched her arm. She held in front of me the book she had been reading. I could read the title: "Reading Lolita in Tehran." It was written by Azar Nafisi, a writer then unknown to me. I came to learn later from Milli that Nafisi taught at Johns Hopkins.

"She will add more bubbles to your cauldron," Milli warned.

I learnt that Azar Nafisi grew up in the shah's Tehran in the '60s. After years abroad, she returned to Iran—the shah had been deposed and ayatollahs ruled. She was stripped of her teaching post at the University of Tehran for refusing to wear a veil—women-fearing mullahs did not tolerate such intransigence. Nafisi went underground. In secret seclusion, she and her students continued to read *Lolita* and *Gatsby*. It was their way of protest.

Milli's voice rose a pitch. "Hear this, Gora. In her book she says adultery is punished by stoning a woman to death, and the legal age of marriage is thirteen, nine with parental consent! Nine, Gora! Nine! Can you believe this?"

"Are you nine yet, Milli?" I asked.

Before I could take that back, Milli countered, "By that liberal math, I am set for my third husband."

She became serious again. "Gora, we need do something

about this."

Obviously Milli had considered the situation and had planned a counterattack. What was she brewing? Civil disobedience? An international boycott of Middle East oil? We would be back in the Dark Ages—literally. Was she sending a petition to all progressive governments to invest their last farthing in alternate energy R&D and thus lower dependence on the ayatollah's oil?

Milli had her own idea.

She said with emotion, "The Americans are sinking deeper in the quicksand. 'Spreading democracy' was Bush's euphemism for a new-age crusade. Now it is Obama's turn."

Crusade was an incendiary word, I thought. Had the time come? Would Jain be able to defuse the dire need for one? I choked my thoughts and turned to *Lolita*.

When I was twelve, my mother walked in on my covert scholarship and caught me reading *Lolita* in a corner of our house, which was infrequently disturbed. She asked me what I was reading. I had said, *Lolita*. Without being rankled, she said, "Oh! That book," or something to that effect. Before leaving me in my seclusion, Mother expressed her confidence in my good judgment. For a woman immersed to her forehead in Hindu tradition, Mother was rather open-minded.

Today Milli raised *Lolita* from erotic discovery to the icon of the rebellious female. "Every Muslim woman should read *Lolita* and burn their yashmak [their headdress] ... Can you believe, Gora, women being lashed for being raped, lashed for driving a car?"

Islamic women's Bastille? The Third War? Ijtihad, the

right of the scholar to reinterpret the *Koran*? Who was the scholar, the mujtahid?

Soliloquy on Ghazu

Muhammad is God's apostle. Those who follow him are ruthless
to the unbelievers but merciful to one another. [Koran 48:29]

Farooq is not given to long statements. Usually his conversation consists of loose phrases linked together by explanatory gestures, like "Coming?" Where to, Farooq? "The usual." Then he would feign being drunk, which meant going to Rajah bar. "Play?" What Farooq? He would gesture with his hand or foot to signal whether he meant soccer or volleyball. Not that Farooq was incapable of an essay. He could narrate a story with great fanfare and emotion. But when a word accomplished as much as a sentence and a sentence as much a paragraph, Farooq elected frugality. So when Farooq's conversation extended beyond a phrase, we expected more than a call to action—we expected a carafe of passion.

Since Jain's disappearance, we visited Rajah's less frequently. Instead, we took long walks on Janpath, sat by the Red Fort ramparts, or strolled around the meadows across from the Jama Masjid. It had been more than five weeks since we saw our professor.

Yuri, Farooq, and I were standing on the balcony in front

of our dorm room watching darkness creep though the leaves of the many sal, teak, and deodar trees that surrounded the Ganges Hostel.

"I am my father's son and so I am a Muslim. I do not pray five times a day. I do fast for the Ramadan. Last month I read Karen Armstrong's *Muhammad*. Jain had suggested it a while back. I now know why he wanted me to read the book. The Bedouin's way of life was ingrained in the Prophet. The Bedouin lived for the tribe; Muhammad's circle is confined to followers of Islam. Ghazu, a raid on another tribe, was acceptable to the Arab. Muhammad never condemned it when he was in Medina."

"Are you turning against Islam?" I asked.

"No. I am not as steadfast as my father. The *Koran* does not discriminate by color or birth. It teaches generosity. I like that. But like the Bedouin around his tribe, the *Koran* draws a circle around Islam. If you are not a Muslim, you are outside the circle. You are alien. You are the object of Ghazu."

"Jain has opened your eyes," said Yuri.

"Yes, I see the good in *Koran*. I also see what is out of time and out of place. My father will disown me for saying this," Farooq Shahjehan admitted. "I am not against Islam. Islam is. Islam must not destroy Islam. There is much good in the *Koran*. The text allows scholarly revision. Ijtihad! Renew what is faded. But who will do it? Which mullah will give up his own power and risk his own life to save the many?"

"Are you on for the ten o'clock news on NDTV, Farooq Mian? That was marvelous. I never would guess so much wisdom grows behind that goatee." Yuri was obviously impressed.

I considered Farooq Shahjehan a colorful young man. The

soliloquy surpassed my expectations.

After Farooq's tirade ended, he paced the balcony with his hands behind his back. Yuri could not resist. He mimicked Farooq, placed his hands behind his back, and walked back and forth behind Farooq. He stopped pacing suddenly. He became serious.

"You know what I think," Yuri said. "Jain is looking for the answer to your very question. Mark my word, Farooq."

"And the answer is a ten-day week imitating the Jacobins! If there is no Sunday, there is no church!" Farooq mocked.

Chapter 4, Verse 34

As for those [wives] from whom you fear disobedience, admonish them, send them to beds apart and beat them. Then if they obey you take no further action against them.
Surely God is high, supreme. [*Koran:* Chapter 4, verse 34]

Although Jain had great respect for the teachings of Jesus, he held the view that all scriptures are inherently apocryphal. The passage of time and the writ of many hands have buried unintended or deliberate alterations in the process of recreating the sacred texts.

"I have read scholars argue convincingly that numerous accounts of the *Bible* are embedded with changes made in various monasteries. Divine revelation was translated and reassembled bit by bit. It is reasonable to conclude that scribal errors similar to those in the testaments would be present in other texts including the *Vedas* and the *Koran*," he emphasized.

I brought this up with Farooq as the two of us headed toward the Jama Masjid two weeks after his soliloquy. Farooq straightened his Fez as the wind across the steps of the masjid tilted it to one side. "I remember that." That was Farooq's terse answer. Farooq, who can be flippant one minute and intense the next, cleared his throat as we climbed the steps to the square above. I did not know what to expect in reply.

"Father was upset the other day. He has heard from a friend that a newcomer at the masjid is involved in heated discussions with the other clerics. He apparently supports a Shabana Azmi proposal that women of the faith be not coerced to wear the veil. Mullahs pointed to chapters 18 and 22 which purportedly was clear in its directive that women cover their faces in public. Matters got tense when the newcomer brought up the controversy around chapter 4, verse 34 in particular. Father believes such discussions are anti-Islam." Farooq paused. He wanted to see my reaction.

Two thoughts raced through my mind. Who is this young cleric who has the courage to discuss what must be discussed? How could I avoid offending Farooq?

"Even if the rigid control over one's wife had a modicum of relevance in ancient Arabia in Muhammad's time, surely it is out of place today," I said.

"Father says the young man is straight as an arrow but totally off the mark. He argues that several chapters in the *Koran* should be reinterpreted. He pleads with the imam for his permission to debate this in public. Muhammad himself would have surely done so," Farooq replied.

"Like Martin Luther's Reformation in sixteenth century Germany," I said.

"The group was in an uproar. The newcomer had shouted above all others, 'In the name of God, the compassionate, the merciful. Ijtihad! Ijtihad! Ijtihad! Remove the veil from women and the blindfold from your own eyes.' It is a touchy subject."

Farooq went on, "When the group quieted down, the new scholar had said, 'More than a matter of women lifting the purdah, it is about anyone being able to lift his or her voice.' My father is torn between obedience and good sense. The imam has not given his verdict about this."

"Could the newcomer be Jain, our teacher?" I wanted to ask Farooq.

"Father says the imam too is orthodox. He can't support the newcomer's viewpoint wholeheartedly. But my father thinks that the imam likes the young man. He has instructed the guards to protect the newcomer. A nod from the imam could have immense consequences." We had reached the last step up as Farooq finished his account.

Up in the openness of the square, I asked, "Farooq Shahjehan, tell me what you think. Is this newcomer Jain?"

Farooq stroked his fine pointed goatee between his right thumb and the index and middle fingers.

I continued more forcefully. "It has to be. Remember the incident I told you about of the man at the far end of the masjid square I thought was Jain? He disappeared before I could get a good glimpse of him. I can't swear it was he. With the pigeons whirling and the seeds flying, I could not be certain. Ask your father. Ask him for his name. Ask him about his height, his built, his eyes! Can your father get us this newcomer's photo?"

"No photos are allowed inside the inner chamber of the mosque, Gora."

"Believe me, Farooq, a poet can feel things. The newcomer is Jain." I was emphatic.

"I too see it." Farooq shook his head. He placed a hand over my shoulder. I knew what crossed his mind. I too was scared.

Sin

Man is enjoined to embrace wuwei—nonaction—letting things happen naturally and responding selflessly to them. [The Tao Way]

There were times though when Farooq was not as certain of our ties with Jain's destiny. "What if we denied Jain and went on with our own lives? Would it be wrong?" he wondered, just another week later.

"Is your destiny tied to Jain's?" I rephrased the question. "I myself have decided to wait. The answer will come to us. Though still in the dark, you and I are part of the plan. The answer lies within each of us."

I was leaning on Jain's staff!

There is an oval fenced-in rock garden with many uncommon plants in front of the School of Art and Aesthetics, a turn away from the tree-lined main road leading into JNU. I sat there one late afternoon, a few weeks after we had joined Jain's Snakes and Ladder lectures, waiting for Milli to join me. A low hanging babul tree with leaves like baby's fingers was Milli's favorite. The branches of a neem tree with its finely crenate pinnate leaves provided me shade. Professor Jain was passing by. On seeing me, he stopped to sit down on the grass beside me. A book on Spinoza was in his hand. I can't recall the author's name. My mind was far from philosophy just then. I was rehearsing the lines that would win Milli's devotion forever. The book must have prompted me. I cannot find any other reason for the question I posed next to Jain. "Can you sin if you believe that there is no God?" It was a trick question forced out of my mouth by my vestigial knowledge of Spinoza. I confess when I think of Spinoza I think of Yuri's criticism of philosophers—wrapping a rope of words around themselves. Free will, God, personal responsibility, and all those difficult connections! I mean if you do not believe in God, who are you sinning against?

What Jain said was this: "I don't know what sin is, Gora. You know I was born to Muslim parents, but I was raised as a Hindu. In our house we did not eat beef. We followed the Hindu tradition. My mother was traditional in her ways. I had heard of Nizam's from some friends. The chef at Nizam's made the best beef rolls, my friends claimed. I asked my mother if it would be sinful if I went to Nizam's with my friends to taste the rolls. My mother said, 'If you think it is sinful, it will be a sin.' Since then I do not think in terms of sin or otherwise. I think of my actions as right or wrong."

After Jain left and Milli came, I related this story to her. "If you think it is sinful, it will be a sin."

"Religion in a nutshell," she said.

The Oracle and the Fugue

What heaven has conferred is nature; accordance with this nature is the path of duty;
the regulation of this path is the instruction ... till you know about the living, how are you to know about the dead? [Confucius]

Our repeated attempts to find Jain at the mosque over the next few days were futile. However, our suspicion that the young upstart cleric at the mosque was indeed our Professor Jain was turning to a more positive "it has to be; it can't be otherwise." We had asked the guards point-blank, describing Jain's physique, his features, the pitch of his voice, and each detail that could lead to a firm recognition. None of the guards we spoke to had ever seen such a person. One guard's denial was unusually vehement.

"More than half the young men in India fit your description. There is no professor here, only holy men."

Perhaps the guard was having a bad day. Yuri diagnosed it as conspiracy.

On a late afternoon in mid July, from the balcony in front of Yuri's room, we watched the egress of the sun soothe the blistered day. Yuri's white skin caught the shadow of the leaves seeking respite from the afternoon light. I wiped my forehead with my shirt sleeve. My mind was tortured by the absence of Jain. Why had he not shared his plans, if he had any, with us yet? Weeks and months had passed since we last heard him speak. What was revealed to him? He had introduced a higher beat to the mixed drone of our humdrum existence. Time passed slowly and painfully for me without his presence, his words.

My spirit sagged like the skin of time, deprived of the balm Jain brought us. If it was not for Yuri's constant vigil over my hopelessness, I would have relapsed into the depression from which he had saved me once before.

"Poetry will age you, Gora," Yuri remarked when I read the poem to him. "Ageless poetry dealt with reality," I argued.

Yuri fanned his face with my poetry notebook. His message: inspirational rhyme was an evanescent breeze that did little to heal the oppression of a hot summer day.

I have felt the skin of Time
grow loose
like my lover's.

I have seen the icy wind
embrace silver-haired weeds
leaning dead on the golden pond.

I have measured Time's busy feet
on round run of the sun—
topple and swoon

and revive—
reborn as the moon
afloat on a boat.

I convinced myself that the man who I thought was Jain, the man I had seen disappear into the inner sanctum of the Jama Masjid, was an illusion. It was an act of faith—a visual hallucination wrought by my intense desire to find Jain again.

As the sun dipped behind the row of houses above the horizon, strange emotions gripped my sanity by the throat. I heard five voices reciting five different themes simultaneously. I remember the polyphonic recitals distinctly. I was determined not to sink into hopelessness, but the harder I tried to make sense out of this weird orchestration, the deeper was my sense of inadequacy.

"Who has draped the moon in a bra? For the seeing eye the star is not far" merged into "Morning chases the night and you and I must arise." Before that line ended "lightning lights the cloud and thirsty petals swallow the rain" and "night is the womb that brings the morning to light" coalesced into "the bird with painted wings will swallow the lightning rod." The last was especially puzzling. These came in rapid repetitious succession, each distinct and yet not separated from one another.

As I related them to him, Yuri tried to make sense of the fugue. He believed that what I had seen at the masjid was real. If we were patient and patiently prepared for the events that would inevitably play out, our blindfolds would be removed in time.

Yuri put his arms around me. "Don't you understand? You are a poet. You are the oracle."

The Last Day of Ramadan

Oracle. The word struck a nerve. I began to visit Jama Masjid every day in the hope that I would run into Jain. Often Farooq or Yuri or Milli accompanied me. On some evenings we all went together. We tried to strike a friendship with some of the guards, hoping one of them would divulge a clue. Friendly coercion was met with cold indifference.

In time, news began to escape the confines of the mosque that a man with unusual powers had become a favorite of the imam of Jama Masjid. These tidbits succeeded in keeping our hopes alive. True, he could not heal with his touch. He could not perform miracles. Yet his presence was so powerful that even those who disagreed with him listened to what he had to say. Some said that he had a vision of Prophet Muhammad—that the Prophet had shared a secret with him. There were several mullahs in the mosque who were opposed to letting him appear before the public. But the imam liked him and protected him. The day would come when the imam would let him share his secret vision with the world, one guard finally confided.

We heard stories. Jain—if indeed this man was Jain as we began to convince ourselves—was holding frequent sessions in the inner sanctum of the mosque. With the permission of the imam, debates—and arguments—took place several times a day. The imam's position was softening. After the Shia-Sunni riots in Baghdad, he had his first misgivings. Now with more Shia-Sunni insurrections, he was softening his stance against the new mullah's arguments. More than how others perceived Islam, Islam had to radically change the way it perceived itself. Many mullahs still remained vehemently opposed to the newcomer's interpretations of the Holy Text and to the permissibility of ijtihad.

The young cleric's growing popularity with a handful of younger mullahs was the cause of consternation for the older, more orthodox believers. One of the guards expressed his fear that the newcomer could be poisoned. He liked the new mullah. He had gone to the meeting group to deliver an important bit of news. When challenged by an orthodox cleric about a specific text, he heard the new mullah reply, "Do I need to gulp the entire river to find the taste in water?" The guard kept repeating this to us—he was apparently very touched by this aphorism.

One ominous note. A cleric had asked the young upstart, "If Americans burn the Koran to avenge September 11, how will you return that insult?"

"A book is more than paper and print and opinion. It is a vessel holding sentiment and hope. Each side must respect the other." This is how the young cleric had avoided the trap.

Weeks had passed since Jain was last seen at JNU. We were crestfallen.

***

A week later Farooq came running to me. I was heading out of a class at JNU. He had news. He had gone home for lunch that afternoon. He heard more from his father about this man with unusual powers who was residing in the Jama Masjid. His father had seen him twice—once when he had gone into the mosque quarters to take measurements for this mullah, again when he delivered two hand-sewn white kaftans to him. On interrogation, his father had described to Farooq a lean man shy of six feet with black beard and piercing eyes. He drew people to himself like a magnet. "That's him, Gora. Piercing eyes! Got to be. Let's go and meet him."

The Last Day of Ramadan

We wasted no time. Milli had gone home. We left a message for Yuri at the dorm, and another on Milli's mobile, and hopped on a bus.

Ramadan had begun several moons earlier.

It was sundown when we reached Jama Masjid. The quadrangle was dark by the time we rushed up the steps. Was our dogged pursuit about to find its reward? I caught sight of the kaftan-clad armed guard captured in my pocket Nikon in one corner of the masjid square. Third time! He was unarmed. Same height. Same demeanor. Same black kaftan. It was he. I ran toward him. Farooq followed. The kaftan-clad guard surprised me with a friendly drawn out, "As-salaam alaikum." He was tall and dark. I touched my forehead with the four fingers of my right hand and bowed my head slightly.

"We have met," I said, still panting from the rush and the excitement.

"I know you too," he said, no longer sounding affectionate! "You have a camera. I know your friends too. You come often. We keep an eye on you. Why do non-Muslims come to the masjid so often?"

We were taken aback. Farooq blurted out, "I am a Muslim and he is a good friend."

"That does not tell me why you come here often, does it?" His voice was stern.

I was relieved he was not carrying the bullet vest across his large chest. We were about to turn around and leave the premises when the man in the Nikon winked. He motioned us to the east end of the balustrade. He turned around to see if we had attracted unwanted attention.

"Your teacher is in danger. It is not wise to ask to see him. He will send you word. I have come from Egypt to keep him safe. My name is Syed Musa." He spoke fluent English. He was bigger than the man I had measured through the camera—in brain and brawn. I scolded myself. How wrong I had been. I had instinctively considered him our enemy—the man who would be Jain's protector. To compensate for my unwarranted misgivings, I shook Mr. Musa's hand with added verve.

For a moment, neither Farooq nor I could find a word to utter. We had found Jain. He was alive. He would see us. Anticipation and trepidation sprung a trap and held our voices captive.

Syed Musa spoke again. "Go to his apartment tomorrow evening."

Godsend!

The Fight over a Riddle

Love is confining; Reason is expansive:
Reason then is the greater love. [Jain]

After Mr. Syed Musa's encouraging words, Farooq and I rushed to Milli's house. Her mother let us in. Pamela seemed to be at peace despite the illness of her husband. She was dedicated to him and that afforded her the tranquil beauty that she carried in her gait, effortlessly and unassumingly. No, Milli's father was not much better.

"Occasionally he will mouth a few words," Pamela said. "The speech therapist refuses to give up. She works with him every day."

"Yes, he is walking a bit more. Steadier gait, yes. No, not now, he is taking a nap." Obviously our rapid fire questions about the doctor's health did not conceal our excitement.

"You young men are not in some sort of trouble are you?" Pamela enquired. At that moment, Milli walked in and spared us from exposing a convoluted explanation.

Yuri was on his way. After he arrived, the four of us held hands and prayed. We did not part company till the following evening. Each one of us recalled what we had learnt from Jain's teachings. Before Jain we had not known spirituality. I was no Confucius. Milli was no sacrificing Mother Teresa. Farooq was not Gibran. Yuri was a scholar in search of his roots. As we talked of Jain, we realized how disparate we were—Milli, Yuri, Farooq, and I. Yet we were headed inexorably toward the same fire. Later in the evening, Sohaila came. She sat quietly and listened to our recollection of Jain's teachings. We were awake into the early hours of morning before we fell asleep on the sofas in Milli's house. Sohaila left before midnight.

"Never underestimate the power of the symbol." That's how Jain had opened one of his Snakes and Ladder lectures.

"Christian friends will not be amused if you profess your conviction that the uncovered bones in the limestone ossuaries in Jerusalem's 1980 discovery are those of Jesus, Mariamene, and their son Judah. They will tolerantly listen to what you have to say, try to hide their dislike for you, and scratch you off their list of friends. But trample on a wooden cross, and the offense is thousand fold more provocative. You will have started a riot," he explained.

As I recall, that is how he started the lecture and this is the gist of what he taught that day. He pulled instances from current affairs—in no particular order. It was the deed and what in our hearts made us do a deed that mattered, he had said. "A tsunami of sorts is gathering pent-up frustration at the bottom of the Atlantic, Pacific, and the Indian oceans.

"In our country, the distrust a Hindu fosters for his Muslim brother and the hatred of the Hindu by the Muslim minority simmers underneath the ash. Remove police protection and the furor will run amuck in the streets of Mumbai, Kolkata, and Delhi.

"In England activists have collected petitions to deny a large mosque a requested building permit. After the July 7 London bombings, the aversion toward the minority sect is understandable. The replay is being enacted in New York's Ground Zero.

"France has banned Muslims from donning the headscarf, a powerful act against a prominent symbol. The tsunami is gathering strength. Let us not look away while the hatred gathers hot lava that will erupt—belching vengeance and flooding the earth with blood."

"Is this a war of religions that I foresee and fear?" Jain asked rhetorically. "It is not just Christians against Islam. Why else will Sunni and Shia kill each other on the streets of Baghdad and the dusty lanes of Peshawar—in daylight, under the cover of night, by the roadside, in the home? Why does a gun blow a brain, a dagger spike the heart, or a vest detonate its cruel depraved fury in the marketplace where men and women find their bread and a bowl of milk? No one is spared. Not the aged, not the women, not the child!"

As I understood Professor Jain, though ostensibly religion is at the root cause of violence, deeper emotions are synapsed in human insecurity—man's inability to comprehend God, to understand His minutely laid plans, the fear of the unknown fate—triggered the confused brainwashed mind to go wildly astray! "It is the curse of the dogma. Dogma confuses the mind. Dogma begins with good intentions and ends in blighted confusion."

"I remember," Farooq recalled, "Jain said that day, 'It is man against man. It is the ignorant seeking comfort in the fabricated truth of religion. Remember Gandhi's words: 'I used to think God is Truth, now I know Truth is God'."

Yuri followed. "Herod did not kill Jesus. Old age did not kill Buddha. By proclaiming that they were divine, their followers killed them. Their lofty philosophies should be written onto floating clouds and not confined to the church choir and the temple walls. Jain spoke of a brewing crisis. Apocalypse!"

Milli pulled open a drawer of her desk. A notebook in hand, she sat down close to me on the sofa.

"You wrote this, Gora. I love it. 'The Magic Man'! Listen."

The magic man speaks in riddles—
curious words that twist the tongue:
"If God is one and man his image,
clearly there are gods too many.
If death is peaceful as is sleep
why is night so long?"

"So much is unknown. Life is a riddle. What a shame we fight over what we know the least about," Milli mused.

Many days had passed since we saw Jain last at JNU. Syed Musa would bring Jain to us. It was difficult to fall asleep that night.

Falling in Silence

Then Job answered the Lord and said, Behold I am vile; What shall I answer thee? I will lay mine hand upon my mouth. [Book of Job]

It was four in the morning. Milli was asleep by three. I was writing a poem at Milli's desk. I could not shut my eyelids. I was scared because I could not see beyond the darkness of the night. I was eager to see daylight. What would daylight reveal? I sipped from a mug of hot coffee I had brewed in the microwave as I reread the poem.

In the center of the equator, past the gate
beyond the arbor wreathed in flowers,
steps give way
under the weight ...
and you fall through silence
alone
through leaping flames
alone
through blinding blizzards
alone
onto the lap of gentle waves—
and then there are others.

I concede I was falling through the silence, the flames, and the blizzard. I tried hard to recall everything Jain had said and taught in and outside class. Instead of falling on the gentle lap of waves, I was being sucked into a tempest. Each wave took me farther from the shore. Was Jain trying to save the world with four disciples with few common goals besides friendship? He would be better off with fishermen! Self-aggrandizement? But Jain was naturally unpretentious—in clothes, in habits, in the clarity of his thought. I was confused.

I was still falling in silence when Farooq said, "Make me a cup. I can't fall asleep."

He had been silent all this time. I had thought he was asleep.

Yuri woke up while I made coffee. He too was uncertain of what was to come. The leopard of a Russian, who when he walked the streets of Delhi people made way to let him pass, even he kept coming back to the word destiny like a caged parrot.

"He has chosen us, Gora. Why else would I be in Delhi and not in Moscow?"

"The Age of Kings followed the Age of Hunters. The Fourth Empire will follow the Age of Bigotry," recalled Yuri. "The Fourth Empire that surely must come."

"What the Prophet had taught in the darkness that prevailed over the desert one and a half millennium earlier was what men and women could digest then. This is the dawn of an Enlightened Age—the Age of Truth, The Fourth Empire. The prophet would have new teachings for men and for women of the twenty-first century," Jain had said in class.

Why is this night so long, I wondered.

Breaking Bread

Hear, Israel, the Lord is our God, the Lord is one. And the words I command you today shall be in your heart. And you shall teach them to your children. And you will speak of them when you sit at home, and when you walk along the way, and when you lie down, and when you rise up. [Deuteronomy]

It was nine when we awoke. We must have dozed off in the wee hours of the night. Pamela walked in. She had asked the cook to prepare a breakfast of tea, toast, and scrambled eggs.

"You are up to something!" Pamela teased.

When I attempted to explain, she said, "I know, I know. Milli tells me everything."

After breakfast, Farooq, Yuri and I returned to the dorm and waited impatiently till it was dusk and time to go to Jain's flat. Our instruction from Syed Musa was to "be there after the street lights are turned on."

Sohaila had come too. She wore a blue salwar-kameez today, the color of the morning sky.

Milli embraced her. "You look pretty."

In her turn, Sohaila admired Milli's ponytail.

Farooq pulled on my shirt sleeve, pointed to Sohaila, and meaningfully lipped the word silently "women."

I was tense. I managed to bring forth a waning smile.

We said very little.

Once Farooq asked, "What if I can't do what Jain asks for?"

We remained silent.

Minutes later Yuri tried to make the air light.

"I am glad to be here and not in Moscow. In Moscow I would be drinking Putin's cocktail: vodka, rooster's blood, crushed newsprint, Gazprom's residue, a dry olive branch."

We waited. Yuri untied and retied the red bandana around his neck. He paced up and down the verandah with nervous energy.

"In anthropology progress is replacing old prejudices with new ones. What if …?" His pace picked up speed.

"Slow down, Yuri! Perhaps all Jain wants to say is goodbye." I too had my doubts.

Street lights had come on half an hour ago. A black sedan stopped in front of the building. The headlights went off. The doors remained closed, the windows down several inches up front. Nothing moved! Three minutes later, a man in a dark pinstriped suit came out of the driver's side of the car. It was Syed Musa. He held open the back passenger door.

A man in khaki trousers and a white shirt came out of the backseat. His beard was bushy and long, ending in a thick point like an artist's brush. It was Jain!

Mr. Musa said something to Jain before he got back in the car and drove away. He parked on the opposite side of the street and turned off the lights. We did not see him come out of the car.

Jain looked up. He saw us leaning over the balcony. He smiled as he entered the building.

My fingers trembled as I held open the door to Jain's apartment. Yuri noticed it. He hugged me. Sohaila and Milli held hands. Farooq paced in front of the elevator shaft, which was only ten feet away. When Jain came off the elevator, I stayed at the door. The others rushed to greet him.

I looked at him: his face, his beard, his eyes. He was gaunt—much thinner than when we had last seen him. His beard was thick around his face—black, curled, and ending in a rounded point. We poured our questions into his soul—silently.

We followed Jain into the apartment. He sat at the dining table and we around him.

He began, "I have kept in touch with you though you have not known it. Your work starts soon. Our mission is planned. You will help me carry it out. The world is boiling over. No place is safe. Not America, not Europe, not Asia. There is danger of a great war."

He sipped from a glass of water. "People look at each other suspiciously before they take their seat on a plane or a bus. We mistrust the man sitting at the next table in a restaurant. Before the powder keg spreads more mayhem across the globe, we must prevent it."

Jain broke a loaf of bread. He had brought the loaf with him. This he shared with us. This done, he filled a glass with water. He asked us to sip from it in turn. After he had taken the last sip, Jain went round the table and embraced each one of us, placing his right hand on our forehead and blessing us. He was pleased that Farooq had brought Sohaila along.

As he placed his hand on her forehead, he said, "We will need you and all your friends."

After he sat down again, he placed his clasped hand in front of him on the table. This is what we had waited for eagerly—for days, for months.

"I promised to reveal to you what the Prophet Muhammad had said to me in my vision. The day has come to let the world know. On the last day of this Ramadan, there will be a gathering at the Jama Masjid. You will spread this word. Gather your friends and neighbors. Speak to everyone you meet, on the road, at the bus stop, in the university. Ask them to help you spread the notice of this gathering. Print pamphlets. Spread your message on the Internet. Go to the press. Syed Musa, who drove me to the flat today, will provide all the funds you will need. He has the support of men who share our view."

Farooq asked pointedly, "Who is this Syed Musa? Where did you find him? He carries an AK. Gora saw him with one. We met him at the masjid. He drove you to your apartment. Is he our true friend, your follower?"

"He is our instrument. He who helps us spread the word of change, he who helps us accomplish our mission of peace, is on our side. He is employed by a tycoon who desperately wants us to succeed," Jain said softly.

After a pause, he said, "I will speak to the people on the last night of Ramadan. Spread the word by word of mouth, by pamphlets, by blogs on the Internet that there will be a gathering at the Jama Masjid. Reveal that the message comes from the Prophet. Crowds will come. Be there. Do not reveal my identity. I am in grave danger. The mission might fail if I am revealed before the last night of Ramadan. It is but a fortnight from today."

Jain continued, "The secret must be guarded as sacred.

When the sickle moon rides over the sky, on the evening of the last day of Ramadan, I will speak to the people. Many will come. Ask the women to come with their hijab, the veils that hide their face and steal their individuality. You will hear what I say. You have waited patiently to know how we plan to carry out our mission. After Ramadan and the festival of Id, spread the word wider. Our cause is great. Never has the name of God been uttered with greater reverence."

Jain then revealed to us what had been revealed to him while he was deep in sleep lying at the bottom of the cliff. As he received his message, the sun had risen over the Himalayas and lit up the world.

We had fifteen days to prepare.

Hijrah

Togetherness breeds fondness, and fondness leads to pain;
since pain issues from fondness wander alone like a rhinoceros. [Buddhasutra]

The buzz on the social media grew louder each day. The news of the planned gathering at the Jama Masjid grounds attracted attention of the media and everyday people on the streets of Delhi. There were whispers of jihad and ijtihad, of strife and salvation. There was confusion and curiosity.

We spent hours each day near the mosque, distributing leaflets about the gathering. At JNU we asked other students to help us spread the word. The air was charged.

People who came to the mosque singly, in pairs, or in small groups—Muslims and Hindus alike—were curious about the planned meeting. There was excitement on their faces—and fear. They heard of the young mullah who had found favor with the imam. Why else would the imam allow a young man to take the center stage? Rumors and facts were inseparable. One heard that the young cleric was indeed a learned man, a professor. Some said the young man had magical powers—that he could make a blind man see. Surely he must have healing powers. Why else would the imam let him speak to the crowd? Some accused the man of being a sorcerer who had won influence with the elders with magic, deception, and yes, bribes!

Regular worshippers at the mosque said that it was the young cleric who would be introduced but no doubt the imam would have the last word. The imam was a respected and powerful man. The messenger in the leaflet would introduce the topic but it would be the imam who would hold the night.

As words began to leak out that women were being invited in droves, theories of conspiracy by the government began to circulate. The air was charged. No, said others, the imam would not stand for any government meddling.

There was as much speculation about the message as about the messenger. There was curiosity about the man and the events that were to unfold. No one knew with any degree of certainty what was about to happen. Police were on alert.

There was fear. There was hope.

Leaflets were circulated asking men and women to come to the masjid at sunset on the twenty-ninth of the month. Women were asked to bring their yashmak, their chadors. There would be prayers. The imam too would address the crowd himself. The chosen day was the end of Ramadan when Muhammad had fled from Mecca to Medina. At the end of Ramadan, with the new beginning of Eid alFitr the day after, their bodies fed, their souls would be nourished. They would receive new teachings. The Prophet would bless the crowd.

The pamphlets mentioned the messenger but not his name. Some who had sources at the mosque were fearful of a conspiracy. If indeed the name of the mullah was Jain, he could not be a Muslim! Others argued that Kabir Humayun was not a Hindu name, if indeed that was his real name!

Some said the Prophet himself would come, others that he had chosen a new disciple. Some went so far as to say that a new savior—who had been born and raised in the mosque—and who had never set foot beyond the premises, would soon reveal himself to the people.

We did not see Jain at the mosque.

Syed Musa whispered to us, "He has been taken where he will be safe. I don't know where he is. But I know he is safe. There are factions opposed to his plan. They want him dead."

Musa repeated "He is safe" thrice before adding, "Powerful men like what Jain has to say. They want to spread his word. Allah will keep Jain safe."

We worked with the energy of a squirrel who has found a mound of walnuts. Sohaila went from door to door talking to people at home and at their workplace. Farooq distributed leaflets in Old Delhi. I approached many at the university. Yuri and Milli sent messages through cyberspace.

Newspapers began to pick up the story. The imam refused to be interviewed by journalists. This encouraged more publicity—and inevitably more speculation. Several times we heard that the government was going to ban the event.

Ramadan, the days of fasting, had begun on the last day of July. Farooq and Sohaila kept their fast—from daybreak till the sun went down. Each day we went about our mission without betraying what Jain was to reveal on August 29—the night of destiny.

The Night of August 29: How Kabir H. Jain Became a Deity

This I ask thee, tell me truly, Ahura.
Who upheld the earth beneath, and the firmament from falling? [Zarathustra]

The masjid facade was ablaze with a million megawatts of light. The surrounding city looked dim and dark in contrast. People overflowed from the mosque onto the grounds below. Women were allowed to pass and gather in the square till the quadrangle was filled with people and not one more could be squeezed in. We had gone in early and found a place on the rampart not far from the inner sanctum in the right rear of the quadrangle. The crowd was unusually quiet and disciplined. Policemen guided the people with little coercion to form rows around the mosque. The expectation of great things had mesmerized the crowd.

It was a mixed crowd—mostly Muslims, but there were Christians and Hindus and Sikhs with their distinctive turbans. Youth intermingled with octogenarians; young girls stood alongside their mothers and aunts.

"I never expected to see so many people. I was afraid no one would show up," remarked Sohaila.

"Don't you get it? During those agonizing weeks after his disappearance, Jain was working on this from the inside,"

Farooq said.

Orange and blue flames leapt upward from the fire that burnt in the center of the quadrangle. Rows of guard rail were around the small square where the fire burnt, cordoned and protected by men in white clothing. People waited patiently as darkness snail-paced over the landscape. The sun leaned to the west and would soon be lost in the belly of the night. Stars would light the sky—such was the hope of the crowd who prayed silently where we stood beside the rampart. This was to be a night of miracles.

Ramadan ended this day as the new moon appeared—a silver talisman against the dark sky. The Prophet received the *Koran* from heaven during the holy month of Ramadan. Many in the crowd had come to these grounds the night before—Laylat alQadr, the Night of Power. Tonight was different. The crowd was larger. The air was heavy. Many thousand zealous eyes searched the sky with eager anticipation.

A rope of gray cloud hung from the crescent moon. Wisps of lighter cloud floated past the nascent moon. As it grew darker, the horizon caught the color of the burning fire turning yellow and orange and brown in unpredictable succession. At a distance to the northeast, the brick walls of the fort appeared eerie—tungsten shadows and light on rugged brick walls hurled ineffectively against the opaque night.

The sun had set an hour ago. The crowd was shifting on its feet. Signs of restlessness began to spread across the gathered. Then as if on command, the crowd turned to look to the northeast. From where we sat on the rampart, we saw a cone of light rise from the ground near the fort. At first indistinct, the distant roar of a helicopter strengthened as it approached the gathered crowd. The precisely timed lights on the fuselage blinked threateningly. The cone of light from the underbelly of the craft drew a brighter circle as it approached the mosque, stepping over houses, trees and buildings as it came closer. It was now less than half a mile away. The crowd kept its gaze riveted on the approaching helicopter, emitting repeated gasps in anticipation of the celestial drama unfolding and the message they were promised to receive from the giant in the sky—the Nephilim.

As the drone of the helicopter grew louder, the crowd became quieter. The helicopter was headed on a bird's eye flight from the direction of the fort toward the mosque where the crowd was gathered. We had expected to hear messages broadcast over loudspeakers announcing the coming of the copter. There were none.

The helicopter was now within several hundred yards of the mosque. The crowd's gaze was fixed on its path. Instinctively, I looked back toward the inner sanctum of the masjid. I spotted the man in black kaftan with the blue and white scarf around his head. Buttressed against the far corner of the square, he appeared taller than the crowd around him. He must have stood on a platform. I could not see it. He held a weapon in his arm. Was it the Kalashnikov that once before had scared me to death? Once again fear gripped me. I pointed him out to Yuri. In the light from the flames, he flickered on and off like a neon figure at a circus entrance. It was he—the man in my pocket Nikon—Syed Musa. I could see him framed by the entrance arch to the inner sanctums.

Syed Musa stood tall and erect. His eyes were riveted to the approaching helicopter. I recalled how he had escorted Jain to his apartment after his long absence from the university and from our company. I was peeved by my misplaced distrust. He began to look comforting—very different from his menacing pose in my Nikon shot. I strained to see if his fingers were on the trigger. He was far off. I could not see his hands. Nevertheless, he was there to protect Jain if the crowd turned rowdy and violent.

I took my eyes off Syed Musa and turned my attention back to the approaching helicopter. It was now less than a hundred yards from the mosque. From the far corner of the mosque, a loudspeaker announced, "Allah Ho Akbar" thrice. Then there was a plea for the crowd to remain quiet. The truth would be revealed to them. They should do as instructed. "Allah Ho Akbar" filled the night air as the crowd echoed the holy chant. Then there was silence. This announcement followed: "Stay in your places. God's message is being brought to you." The message came from the loudspeakers on the masjid grounds, not from the helicopter.

The copter, now fifty yards from where we were, leaned forward toward the quadrangle. The rotor tips rotated faster, the roar grew louder, and the gusts of forced wind were uncomfortably stronger. Wisely, Farooq refrained from a futile attempt to retrieve his fez. Milli shouted into my ear. I could make nothing of it. The noise from the heli drowned all other sounds. Yuri made the sign of the cross. Habit!

The helicopter was now overhead, suspended above the crowd, rocking with a gentle seesaw motion. The insignia on its side—a soft silver crescent moon holding a mellow orange sun—was visible in the light of the fire burning directly below

The Last Day of Ramadan

the copter in the center of the square. A loud voice over a mike came from the helicopter as it hovered safely above the flames.

The voice from the overhead helicopter was surprisingly clear and distinct over the purr of the helicopter. A few in the crowd turned to look northeastward toward the fort. I followed their gaze. I saw a second helicopter circling the fort. It was at a safe distance—perhaps an army helicopter keeping surveillance over the gathering—a peremptory but routine security measure. I pointed it out to Yuri. He made the sign of the cross—again!

"Hear the word of the Prophet. These are his edicts. The word of the *Koran* asks men and women to be good to themselves and to each other. Men and women are proclaimed equal from this day hence. The God of Islam has revealed that what was true fifteen hundred years ago must change with the time. When this night ends, the world will awake to a new morning. This is the Age of Truth, the Age of New Frontiers. Men and women will leave the earth and travel to distant lands. Jihad is an old word, a misused word. It no longer belongs in the Holy Text. There is no salvation in killing. Both men and women are free. This is the Age of Freedom for everyone. The Prophet instructs each Muslim woman to burn her hijab, her niqab, the black veil that hides her inner loveliness, in the fire that he has lit for you. A Muslim woman will read and learn and be equal to man. She will stand shoulder to shoulder with him, his equal friend and partner."

It was the voice of Jain!

The crowd began to stir. Women near the center of the square threw their niqabs and hijabs into the fire. Those farther off began to hurl them toward the burning flames, which became brighter and leapt higher. The helicopter seesawed gently over the crowd. The crowd was shouting, "Allah Ho Akbar!" In ecstasy, their hearts were touched by the voice that rose above the drone of the rotors and fell from the sky, men and women strained their arms toward the copter. They wanted to touch the man in it, to be lifted to it by divine magic.

Nephilim!

The voice from the helicopter spoke again—distinctly and loudly.

"Let your neighbor come to your house of worship. With love in your heart, you in turn go to his and pray to his God. His God is your God. There is one God, and he is the God of all men and all women. All are equal in his eyes. There is one God and there are many books. Who would you rather choose: the One God or a book? Do not put a veil over your woman's eyes. So says the Prophet. A woman must be true to her man and a man to his woman. He forbids killing in his name. He forbids jihad. This is his decree, his Ijtihad."

The second copter that I had seen circling the fort was now headed toward the masjid. It was now five hundred yards away. The whirring of its rotors grew louder and more frightening, but the hungry crowd, sustained by the manna that fell from the sky, paid scant attention to it. Women continued to fling hijabs and niqabs into the fire. Sparks rose from the fire and dissipated into the air above. I looked back to observe that Syed Musa's rifle was pointed at the approaching helicopter. Yes, he was there to protect Jain. But why the second copter? What was its mission? I shook Farooq and Yuri by their shoulders. They too had been surprised by the approach of the second helicopter.

The helicopter above the square stayed in its position, rocking gently above the fire below. Jain's voice was loud but less clear, partly drowned in the helicopters' whirring blades. The approaching helicopter lunged forward toward the square. It was still a few hundred yards away. It caught the crowd's attention with that push forward. A collective gasp came from the crowd, its discipline now frail. Restlessness spread though the crowd. Instinctively, I grabbed Milli's arm and drew her close to me. Farooq was about to run. Yuri pulled Farooq back.

The voice from the helicopter was heard again. This time the voice was high-pitched and vibrant. It was Jain again.

"Do not let fear rule your lives. God has given you reason; he has given you love. With both love and reason, you will hear the voice of God in the silence of the night. Remember this when you see the sun at dawn. The Prophet condemns jihad. He has spoken. I have heard him. You too will hear this when you open your heart and mind to the truth ..."

I turned again to look back. Musa's rifle was now pointed directly at the helicopter that hovered over the masjid quadrangle. I saw Musa hesitate a moment. He pointed his rifle at the fire. Then he took aim and began to fire at the copter above as it rocked above the fire—the copter above us from which Jain spoke! Has he gone mad! Has he forgotten who he is to protect? I was bewildered. I froze. The volley of gunfire hit the helicopter above us. It began to spin out of control.

There was disorder. The crowd began to flee the square. Some jumped over the rampart. The stampede had begun. Shrieks and groans tore the night sky.

I held Milli's hand tighter. I told her to stay put. It was dangerous to run with the crowd. Farooq's eyes were transfixed on the helicopter. He was muttering a prayer. Yuri kept repeating "Vey iz mir … Woe is me … Vey iz mir … Woe is me …"

The second helicopter was over the crowd spread around the masjid. It turned in a threatening arc around the masjid thrice. Once the volley of rifle shots tore the tense air above the crowd, it turned one last time in a wider, more intimidating tilt before it roared back beyond the fort and disappeared into the distant darkness.

"Vey iz mir. Woe is me. Vey iz mir. Woe is me." Yuri was still praying. Another frantic volley of gunfire hit the copter above us. A rotor blade came loose and flew into a corner of the square. There were cries and wails from that corner. The crowd began to jump over the low balustrade. People trampled over others to flee the square.

The helicopter struggled overhead. The cone of light was extinguished. The fuselage lights went off. The rotors froze and the copter plunged in a nightmarish spiral and crashed onto the fire in which women had burnt their yashmaks. I shouted "Jain!" and rushed forward. I fell within a few feet of the fire.

I must have passed out. When I came to, Milli was shaking me by the collar of my shirt. "Gora! Are you okay, Gora?"

The crowd had regrouped in the open spaces around the masjid, safely away from the burning copter. Ambulance sirens filled the dome of air above the mosque. Crackles from the burning metal reminded me that in it lay Jain. In the moment of ascension Jain had atoned for the sin of others—he would burn so others could live.

Someone was speaking into a hand-held loudspeaker. "Jihad is dead." It was Yuri. He shouted this refrain over and over again. Then the crowd joined him in a deafening chorus. "Jihad is dead. Jihad is dead. Jihad is dead."

Yuri now changed the refrain. "Jihad is dead. Jai Sant Kabir Jain. [Victory to Saint Jain]."

The crowd caught on. They began chanting, "Jihad is dead. Jai Sant Kabir Jain ... Jihad is dead. Jai Sant Kabir Jain ..."

"Ijtihad! Ijtihad! Ijtihad!" rang through the night sky. It was Farooq's voice.

The chanting grew louder and spread across the night sky on radio and television. The rope of cloud around the crescent moon faded and left the crystal moon without blemish.

I recalled, as if directed, "Night is the womb that brings the morning to light."

Epilogue

Two days later, I was recovering from the burns I suffered on August 29, the last night of Ramadan. I stayed off the pain pills as much as I could to stay in touch with the disciples. Between her bursts of sobbing, Milli kept me abreast of the news, of the people, and of our mission: to spread the message of tolerance and of honest ecumenical acceptance that religion is the teaching of great men and not divine revelation.

Yuri came up to me holding a pamphlet in his hand. I recognized it instantly. It was a copy of The Passages, the pamphlet Professor Jain had handed out to his students. The red bandana across his forehead was soaked with sweat. Yuri tried to suppress his excitement lest it make me ill. Keeping his voice low and his emotion in check, he informed me that the word of Jain's sacrifice was out on the airwaves, on Twitter pages and blogs. The press was covering the story with banners. Yuri was interviewed several times. Not just the Indian papers, but newspapers everywhere in the world were covering what happened on the night of August 29. Law enforcement had been quick to cordon the house and business establishments of Mr. Z, the tycoon. The word was he would be charged with mass murder. Mr. Z was in hiding. No one knew his whereabouts. His secretary denied all knowledge of the attack on Jain's helicopter. Some say Mr. Zakiruddin left for Yemen on the night of August 29.

There were many other rumors.

Jain, the helicopter pilot, and twelve others died that night. It could have been a worse catastrophe. It is by God's grace that more people were not killed. Many were injured. Syed Musa, the Egyptian, was taken into custody. Rumor had it that he had ties to the Brotherhood.

I listened to what Yuri had to say. I thanked him, hoping that would set him at ease. He could not contain himself any longer. Seeing how tightly he gripped the pamphlet in his hand, the tendons taut over his knuckles, I knew Yuri too had deciphered what we would have discovered months ago had we had stronger faith in our teacher.

"Gora!" he whispered. "Look at this, the first page of the pamphlet. See here. On the first page, the first words! Remember the last day we saw him at his flat? I understand now why he said to us, 'Read *The Passages*.' I should have known it all along. The fool that I am!" Yuri slapped the back of his hand with the pamphlet thrice. "The fool that I am."

The last tarot card! O The Fool! I relived the séance. Who is wise? Who is the Fool? He who lives or he who gives? I saw Jain on the tarot card holding the staff I had given him, treading steadfastly beyond the precipice. Also I remembered were my own words: "Greatness is its own guide."

"You are no fool. He wanted it this way. He loved the men on the street. For them he would give all he possessed. Remember the boy in Kinari Bazaar? I was certain you would discover this—you are the scholar. I too have realized—the first words of the quotations, the first six, on the first page of *The Passages*."

⇧ ⇧ ⇧

The journey from the small town of Munger in India to Baltimore,
on the way stopping for varying periods at Patna, Kolkata, New York, Kankakee in Illinois,
has the contents of a travelogue.
As I transition from a doctor dedicated to caring for patients to a full-time writer,
I feel the excitement I felt years ago as I crossed the oceans to enter a new continent.

—Gandharva raja

About Gandharva raja

Gandharva raja, aka Dr. Tapendu K Basu, a Nephrologist, is a member of the American Academy of Poets and the Rotary Club. He is the author of *August 29: How Kabir H. Jain Became a Deity; Epic Mahabharata: A Twentieth Century Retelling;* and *Hoofbeats: A Poetic History of the United States.* His novel *The Nisha Trilogy* was produced as a Bengali  movie 'Tadanto'(investigation) in Tollywood. He has completed his parallel novel *I, Kanishka* which awaits publication. He is a member of the Baltimore Chapter of the Maryland Writers' Association and Editor of *Pen In Hand*, its literary journal…

Coming soon...

The lives of common men and women are not eulogized in historical texts. Yet they are the bricks and mortar with which an empire is built. Too, the peasant and the artisan possess emotions that run parallel to the emperor's, though not on the same grand scale.

In the second century, the Kushan Emperor Kanishka, a contemporary of Roman Trajan and Hadrian, ruled over a vast empire in Central Asia including Afghanistan and north India.

I, Kanishka: The Author and the Emperor

is the parallel fictionalized story of the life, victories and struggles of the Emperor, and his namesake, an aspiring New York author.

Agony and the ecstasy weaves through both lives, that of the Emperor Kanishka, and Kanishka, the struggling writer.

Weaving historical events, Gandharva raja has painted the life of the Emperor, his wives, his citizens, his triumphs and his tribulations. After a troubled marriage ends, in a daring bid, the author Kanishka travels to Peshawar in Pakistan to conduct research on the life of his namesake Emperor. He is captured and placed in captivity.

Events move with fast pace and end in a theatric finish, the death of the Emperor and the Author's return to New York.